C000260251

CONTENTS

SILKE THE CAT

. . . .

MY STORY

AS DICTATED TO
GRAHAM AUSTIN
AND BOB ABLE

THIS BOOK IS DEDICATED TO ME, OF COURSE!

Silke the Cat

PREFACE

Bob Able is a best selling author and became fascinated by the wealth of adventures his friend **Graham Austin** had enjoyed with his remarkable cat, **Silke**.

The three decided to draw together Graham's notes and Silke's reminiscences to produce a record of their experiences.

Silke, of course, took the lead and the result is this lighthearted book.

We hope you have as much fun reading it as we had writing it.

INTRODUCTION

Ah human, I see you have decided to make the wise decision and look at my book to understand a little about a cat and to learn about my adventures. Sensible choice, if I may say so ... and of course I may, because this is my story after all.

If you read with due diligence and care, you will gain an insight into, not just my thoughts, but those of Cat-kind and, as a bonus you will be able to enjoy my adventures as a rather attractive cat with superior intelligence and outstanding experience of travelling, with my doting human, across Europe from my home in Spain.

This book will provide you with an insight into how other, less fortunate cats live in countries such as Britain and France, for example, who (or should that be 'whom') I have encountered on my travels.

You are fortunate indeed to have stumbled upon this rather special little book, human, because although I say it myself, I am a quite exceptional cat and my adventures are bound to fascinate and amuse. For the paltry cover price (which, if you haven't paid up yet, get on with it; my human needs funds for my treats and basic sustenance) a whole new entertaining and learning experience awaits you.

So snap to it, pay up and dive in; and travel with me as I walk on my lead (I don't do cat baskets) and travel in my cars with my human around the better parts of Europe.

We will explore the world beyond my territory, staying in hotels, guest houses and other human's homes; and engage with cats, people, and even the occasional dog.
We will share my time in charge of a construction site, and visits to vets, restaurants, woods, mountains and streams as far away as the Pyrenees, and then on to England via the Channel Tunnel.

My human, acting as chauffeur (because I choose not to drive) is assisted, if only slightly, by his human author friend acting as scribe and they may also add a comment or two herein *(in italics)* as we go along. Although I have not read these bits myself ... why would I? ... they won't be as interesting as what I have to recount; I forgive them because humans are like that and can't resist interfering.

Nevertheless enjoy what follows and don't hesitate to send me treats whenever the fancy takes you.

Silke the Cat

THE HUMAN PERSPECTIVE
The beginning

Silke first came to my notice in 2014.

She was discovered by a friend of mine named Cachita, who is an estate agent and was renting a house nearby to a French man with a Spanish wife.

It was a small villa and had a pool. The people who owned it wanted Silke "fostered".

I was wise enough to know this meant 'adopted', as they were moving away.

In fact they abandoned her at the house and Cachita, who adores cats, went round to feed her everyday until she dragged me over to meet her.

"You always said you wanted another cat if you had a garden; well, you have a garden, so you need this cat"…

MY THOUGHTS
Becoming Silke

As you can see, human, I am a particularly attractive cat, and loved by all. But you may be wondering what has happened to my ear. Don't worry, I'm not self-conscious about it, although I admit it does deflect a little from my otherwise immaculate appearance.

When I am in one of my homes abroad, in England, for example, I have noticed that my contemporaries there are not so disfigured. But then they don't, for the most part, have the luxury of my present life or the ability to cross continents at will in one of my motorcars with my pampering human.

You see, human, I have lived, and had a life before my position as top cat was recognised (cats have nine, you know).

I am Silke! Silke is a German's girls name, the German's say Zilka. But my Forever Human says 'SILKA'. Many though, mistakenly call me Silky!

FOUND

Nothing like pressure. Silke was a raggedy thing, smaller than now, under nourished, flea and parasite bitten, and looked very pregnant. She wasn't, its just the way she was made. I took a basket with me knowing she was

coming home with me whatever she was, and was met by a friendly cat who was clearly very sad and broken hearted. She came home with me and I had prepared a bed for her with a dirt box and food bowls ready.

I did not trust her at first as she was very feisty. I wondered if she was feral, so at night she was shut in a small

bedroom downstairs at my villa, which I used as a study in the daytime.

If she did not want to be picked up she would turn into a ball of fury. I even remember one night having to use a broom to sweep her gently into the bedroom because she was so

furious with me for shutting her up in her own bedroom,

albeit with food, water and a dirt box.

I put her in the cattery for Christmas. She really was

too feisty and difficult to trust. When I came home and got her, her attitude had changed completely and she became the Silke we know today. That cattery gave her a time out. But she can still be feisty!

SILKE PICKS UP
THE STORY ...

Has the human finished? Who is writing this?
This is my story!

We cats do not like being shut up in a cat hotel!
Cats are sensitive, you know.
A cat can even learn some words human's use. But
not all. Sometimes we try to say them back but it
is not easy for us, even though of course, we can
make more sounds than a mere dog.
Often the sound of a human voice tells us all we
need to know, from soft kind whispers to shouts.
We don't like lots of noise. Our tails are totally out
of control and
always tell you how our mood is.
Cats *are* moody. Mostly calm, but upset us and we
get angry quickly.
Cats are sensitive creatures, as I said, with ears
that hear better than a human, whiskers that de-
tect movement in the dark and help us to react
fast in a fight. We can smell much better than humans too.

And watch out, because I have teeth and claws to hunt, and fight with.

WHO ADOPTED WHO?

So with a changed cat, and one that did not let me out of her sight after that first cattery visit, Silke started to learn about the car. She always came to greet me, and then she started to jump in for a short journey into the driveway.

So I started making that journey longer; round the block, round the bigger block. At first I did not know if she was happy or not as she yowled so much but since then I have realised it is like a dog barking excitedly.

So I took her further and further, including a motorway, going to a local town and coming back. At first she would yowl and miaow loudly, then she settled down. Over time I got her used to different cars too. Then, heart in mouth, I took her for a walk in the woods at nearby Los Lagos.

Fortunately she followed me! She also responded to my special whistle for her which I had trained her to recognise. Getting her back in the car was a little optional, *her option, not mine, and sometimes she would jump in, sometimes not.*

ONLY A DREAM?

... Negra! people kept saying ... That is Spanish for black....Many people do not like black cats ... I am jet black. I am a cat. My fur does not change anything about me. Except that I can hide in the shadows and pounce on your ankles because you cannot see me!

A rough man, came. I did not like him and when I was near the open door, he yelled at me saying I was

'Mal suerte'...bad luck in Spanish. He chased me out of the house.

I was being chased away by people shouting 'Mal Suerte! Gata Negra!' Bad Luck, Black Cat! in Spanish. Humans seemed to hate me for a reason I did not understand.

Oh no! I was on my own! ....

What's that? ... I beg your pardon, I must have dozed for a moment while the human was yakking on.

I had that dream again.

I have it a lot. It is a memory from one of my past lives.

I don't like it but it won't leave me alone.

Basket case

I realised she wanted to see where she was going. So I had a travel basket made, with a shelf in it on top of which is a soft cushion.

This straps onto the front seat and, in the event of a sharp stop, the basket sides will stop her flying out so easily. She loves it now and knows it means a long journey.

No basket, a short journey.

Then we were ready to do our first trip to the UK that summer.

I had my bright red Mustang over from the USA by this point, and her first UK trip was in that.

ALL IN THE PAST

I also have another dream sometimes. It goes like this ...

... I watched a cat amble down the street, it was obviously on it's own territory. A dog appeared out of nowhere and only at the last minute did the cat know it was in trouble. It got in one swipe of its claws raking the dog before the dog grabbed it by the scruff of the neck and shook it violently!

Given the amount of time we cats spend sleeping, I suppose it is not surprising that we have dreams.

Now where was I?
Oh yes.
I had a feeling about the human when he came to the villa where the lady was feeding me, so I decided to adopt him. Now he is my forever human.

We have had many adventures since then and I travel in his car, sometimes far away from home. But I usually feel safe and I have many adventures to tell you.

I have had my human get a basket made for me so I can see out of the car windows, but hide if I like, too.

TRAVELLING FURTHER

I had also trained her to accept the harness and then the lead. At first the harness meant she just lay on the ground looking furious.

But being a playful puss at times, that mood soon changed, especially when we played with her feather toy. The toy overpowered her grumpiness about the harness. I could often put on her harness after some play like this. Then finally she let me attach the lead.

Having seen someone in a motorway service area with a cat on one of those extending dog leads, and watched the cat go straight up a tree and have to be caught as it was pulled out of it, I knew one of those would be a mistake. Sometimes Silke will walk on the lead, and sometimes not.

She will not be hurried. If you want to do that you pick her up. She will not be dragged. Its almost as though she regards me as the one on the end of the lead being led, not the other way round.

TRAINING

One fateful day my human took me to a cat hotel, shut me in a small cage with my things and left me! Well, it was not *that* small. I could run around and play. My toys were with me. So although I felt sad he had gone, I was fairly certain he would be back. At the cat hotel they came and fed me every morning and night, and in the mornings people came and played with me. Other cats were there too, some coming and some going. All the cats were quiet. No one was claiming territory so there were no fights. The mood was slightly sad. Our own humans were not there, but at least we had food and were dry.

At last my forever human came to get me. When I was in my box in the car I yowled at him loudly. I realised that I must begin training him without delay. But when we were home and he let me out of the box, I made a huge fuss of him and followed him everywhere he went.

He had brought me a new toy; a "flying feather" on a stick!

I had found my forever human. Mine. No one else's.

I love him, but I was glad to be home, and next time I <u>was</u> going with him!

AND COMING HOME

I could sense her relief at being home when we got back from the cattery.

The management there had advised me to provide her with one of my tee-shirts, unwashed for three days for her to sleep with. It seemed to work and gave some comfort as apparently she spent a lot of time sleeping with it. It had certainly helped with 'bonding'.

It was soon after this that she started demanding to come everywhere in the car with me. She would chase the car and, as I drove off, stand in the road with her tail slowly falling; that broke my heart.

She started to leap out into the road to greet me too. I would open the door and she would jump in and ride into the driveway with me. It was around this time she seemed to realise the car was a safe spot, and she had no need to worry if she was in it. I even took her through a car wash to see how she would react … Nothing!

WHAT WE LEARN FROM HISTORY

We had not been home long when a huge tom cat came out of the bushes screaming war at me!

We had a quick fierce fight, I got scratched but I bit him hard, so he came off worst. I walked away, he did too.

No cat really wants to fight. But we will in defence, over food, over territory, and kittens. We don't want to get hurt. But because we are predators and can live by killing mice and birds, we can also scavenge like rats.

That is what this tom cat was doing when I disturbed him. He had found a bin elsewhere, and in it found food. Then, wandering on, he found a little place under MY thick bougainvillea bush and went to sleep off his meal. But this was MY territory, so I was not having that!

When it was over and the human came home he saw my scratches and told me off gently. Humans have so much to learn.

He also started to say something about going on

an adventure.
We were going to a place called France.
No cat hotel for me this time!

HOT STUFF!

On our first long trip, I remember getting close to the border at Perpignan and Silke going for a walk at a services.

She hated the big trucks and their hissing brakes.

We were driving to the hotel 'La Folie'. This meant French 'B' roads at night, and it was really interesting to see how she paid attention to the scenery.

She miaowed a lot when we went through towns. She had spent so much time awake that she was really tired and she insisted in snuggling down on my lap. Normally she understands that, in a car, the driving area is a no-go for her.

When we arrived at La Folie, the proprietor's big dog 'Athos' was very interested in this hissing and spitting little visitor. Silke was not amused at all. However, once inside, she did like our room and settled down immediately.

From that first trip she had taken to sleeping on my bed on occasions and in hotels this is quite acceptable practice, according to Silke.

It was getting hotter and in the morning we took a walk around the woods near the Puilerans Castle ruins, after which we were off again.

Then, somewhere near Toulouse, the air conditioning failed.

INTO FRANCE

I was very interested to see how the scenery changed as we passed from one type of road to another and although some big trucks hissed at me when we stopped for a little walk, it was, on the whole quite enjoyable.

There were places with houses where I really thought the human should stop to explore but he didn't listen to me and just drove on, taking more notice of that woman in the box on the windscreen.

I shouted at her to shut up!

We had been going for a very long time and, although I tried to help the human with my directions, I did get very tired and eventually had to sleep.
The car was quite cold, so, although the human doesn't usually let me go there when he is driving, I curled up on his lap. When I woke we had arrived at a human hotel and, to my horror there was an enormous dog looking at me through the car window!

I hissed and spat and eventually he left me alone and I passed a pleasant night sleeping on the squashy thing beside my human.

Grotty hotels

The next hotel was a grotty little number I had found up near Le Mans.
A real reps special but with a nice steak house adjacent.

We set off in the morning and had an uneventful trip back.

With the air conditioning fixed, some weeks later, we returned, staying at a different rep's special near Le

Mans.

WE ARE GOING ON AND ON!

Staying in a hotel was, of course, a new experience for me, but really quite fun.

I particularly liked exploring the new surroundings in the morning. Since I had trained the human to hold the end of my special lead when I took him for a walk, I was not worried that he would run off, so we had a pleasant stroll through some woods after breakfast.

Then it was back in the car and we drove on again, not back into Spain, but on again, and although I shouted at the woman in the box, she wouldn't listen and we got further and further away from home! It started to get very hot in the car and I was panting. The human was swearing at the car and he had to open the window a bit to cool us down. The car was not listening and it just got hotter and hotter until we got to another human hotel, this time without a dog, where we stopped for the night.

This human hotel was not as nice, but I did have a small portion of steak with my supper.

CHAPTER 2

The cat is in charge

I suppose you might say I am fortunate. I have certainly landed on my feet (we cats usually do) and have adopted a pampering and kind human.

No more than I deserve, of course, but my human is fortunate too, in the things humans value.

He has a large home in a rather better location, considerably smarter than the small domicile where he found me, and outside a large pool for me to drink from encircled by several of those low bed things humans like to lie on in the sun.

I get rather alarmed when he actually gets into the pool and splashes about, going backwards and forwards and getting completely wet. But while he always manages to get out, I cannot understand why he does not learn his lesson and goes in the water again! Still, that is human-kind for you. Not very bright.

He also has several motor cars and can't seem to

make up his mind which one he likes most.

He has a growly red one with a squashy roof which we went to France in, and a quiet and nice smelling one with slippery seats and a picture of some species of cat on the wooden dashboard. But mostly he uses a large, rather posh gold coloured one which has a rattly engine but nice big seats and a wide shelf at the back by a window for me to sit on.

The only problem with this car is that this is where the box woman lives.

When we go for one of our longer drives this annoying woman suddenly starts talking and making unnecessary comments like 'You have arrived at your destination', as if we couldn't see that we were there!
She is very smug.

The human always seems to do what she says and, even when I suggest a detour into a pretty village, or stopping by some interesting looking woods, she will interrupt and tell him where to go.

Perhaps she is his wife. Otherwise how can he bear to listen to her?

Either she is very small and lives in that box or she is curled up inside the car, but I can't find her.

I've been underneath this car many times and looked, but I have never seen her. She seems to live in that box all the time.

How can he stand it? Why doesn't he tell her to be quiet?
I shout at her.
'Shut up!' I say, 'Shut up, box woman!' But she never listens and just spoils our peaceful drives and the scenery with her loud and quite rude interventions.

Don't misunderstand me though, I do especially like this car and, if the human puts my special basket (the one made specially for me with the cushion on the top) on the seat, I know we are going on an adventure.

There is also an even more clattery car which I

don't like but the human loves. It is very old, but shiny and the human seems to have to keep wiping it and getting all sweaty rubbing it with slippery stuff.

It is quite temperamental and grumpy, and gets very hot, but has comfortable seats when it is not moving.

We don't usually go on an adventure in this car, but we do sometimes go up into the mountains in it, wheezing and whining all the way.

I like to be with my human, but I would always rather he took one of the other, more civilised, cars when we go out.

—-oooOOOooo—-

MODES OF TRANSPORT

Silke's attitude to the old Citroen was interesting.

If it's windows or more likely its doors were open she would jump in and make herself at home on the back seat. A regular Princess. However she did not like it moving, and I think found it very noisy. She did like the windscreen being open but really never liked travelling in it. The old '65 Mustang did grumble and roar, she hated that and ran away. She was fine with the newer one though and liked to sit high up on the fabric roof when it was parked. I think she would have liked to ride there on a journey too if she was allowed.

She does not like big trucks. I tried putting her in the cab of one that was visiting the villa once and she came straight out.
On starting up a truck she would bolt. You could not even take her to have a look.
She did however like Pedro, my builder's Ford Transit van, and was in it when he went home for lunch one day. Making her presence known as he got into town so

he had to turn round and bring her back!

THE PROBLEM
WITH POLISH

In the early days, when she had decided she liked travelling in the car, she had learnt that the car can mean walks, not always visits to the vet or the cattery.

One evening I was going out to meet friends. Silke had

been determined to come with me, but of course I could not take her.

I drove the freshly polished Mercedes slowly down the local lanes that lead from the house. Almost at the end of the lane, before it meets the main road, there is a sharp hump back bridge.

I heard a strange sudden 'thump bump' and was alarmed as to what it was. Glancing in the rear view mirror I saw Silke on the road frantically galloping to catch up. She had been on the roof of the car!

I stopped, she jumped in, and I took her home.

Unseen, she must have come out of the cat flap after I was in the car, about to drive off.

I don't ever scold her or shout at her, but I think she had learnt a lesson about riding on the roof of cars. None the less, if she could be on the roof no doubt she would be.

Next best to her is the top of the dashboard.

RIDING ALONG
... TO THE VET!

It took me a while to get the human to understand that I want to go in the car with him and I devised a way of training him whereby I would wait at the end of the drive and turn on my most engaging 'little lost cat' look so that he would stop and open the door for me to get in.

After a few weeks of this he soon got the idea and usually invites me to join him wherever we go.

Sometimes we go to see Rosa.

At first, I didn't like Rosa. She pricked me with a needle and expected me to wait to go in to see her with the common herd in her waiting room.
There were sometimes dogs there, but I chose to ignore them and sat regally on my human's knee with my lead on ... once he realised that I preferred that to being shoved in a box for transportation.

Initially, when I first adopted him, my human

got it into his head that I needed to have nasty white pills hidden in my food or when that failed, pushed down my throat, and it was Rosa who gave him these unpleasant things. Eventually, after several quite angry exchanges about this indignity, the human gave up on it, but started to take me regularly to see Rosa, where she insisted on pricking me again.

I suppose it was her way of saying hello. Humans are difficult to understand sometimes, but on the whole I would rather she pricked my human than me.

I fell asleep once when we went there and had the most awful dream.

It was the one about the dog again, but this time the cat was *me*! Before I could escape this horrible dog had scratched all the fur off my tummy and bitten off part of my ear!

But when I woke up, still with Rosa, it seems the dream had come true … my tummy hurt and the fur had gone and, when I caught sight of my reflection in the side of the shiny cage I was in, my ear had been nipped too!

Perhaps it wasn't a dream and Rosa had rescued me from one of the fierce dogs in the waiting room!

When my human came back, although I was still feeling strange, I yelled at him for leaving me, but

I was much happier to see Rosa after that and I knew she would protect me from the ghastly dogs with their owners outside.

Fortunately she stopped pricking me after that too. Perhaps she only does it until she is sure she has made friends. Odd way to carry on though.

SETTLING IN

When she first arrived, a trip to the vet was necessary.

I had to get her parasite free and check on her general health as well as this potentially pregnant tummy.
On the first visit we hit her with jabs and all sorts. In those days she went in her box.
As is the practice in Spain, the vet clipped her ear after she had opened her up and seen she was already spayed and not pregnant. This easily visible marker prevents feral cats being endlessly bought in to vets by well meaning people to be spayed.
She was so feisty she might still have been feral at that point and we didn't know if she would calm down and become tame.

Poor Silke. She had skin conditions in those days and ripped most of her fur out on her tummy and between her back legs. It was impossible to her give pills and she had no concept that I might be helping her feel better; so it was weekly injections from Rosa.

Somehow she worked out quickly that Rosa was helping her health, but this went on for six months.

WATCH OUT, VET!

Rosa came to the villa as well because she was friends with my human (presumably she had finished with the pricking greeting with him and made friends before she met me).

My human always seemed to be very popular and lots of other humans came to see him, or perhaps me, sometimes in large groups.

I didn't like these gatherings. Too many clumsy people barging about. So I usually sat apart while they got loud, drinking that disgusting stuff they seem to like, and playing noisy music. I was soon busy searching to see if there were any more treats dropped for me to find on the floor.
Involved as I was with a tasty piece of ham some clumsy clot had let slip earlier in the evening, I didn't see Rosa come over. She startled me and became overly familiar; So I bit her!

I was sorry the moment I did it, I don't know what came over me. If it had been any of the other loud humans there it wouldn't have mattered, but Rosa is my friend, and I had to apologise.

Of course I am a very charming cat, one of the very best, actually; and with me it was the work of a moment to repair the damage, and she soon forgave me. But it was a slip-up I regretted deeply, none-the-less.

On one occasion, after she had pricked me, Rosa wrote in a little book which my human gave her. She said the little book was very important and, like this one, was all about me!

On our next adventure my human showed the book to all sorts of people when we stopped the car. They all seemed to like it and looked at me, standing up at the dashboard, and smiled.

I hope lots of humans like this book too!

—-oooOOOooo—-

MORE PROBLEMS

The next trip we made together was, I think, in the Mercedes. It was Christmastime and for some reason I was trying to do the journey in two days.

First to La Folie, my favourite hotel on the route, and then straight to the Channel Tunnel was the plan.
On the way the transmission just disappeared. Hazards on ... I was in road works of course, late at night surrounded by trucks, and had to find a slot to dive between them for the hard shoulder before the car stopped rolling altogether.

Now what.

Cat. Heavy traffic, Christmas time, late at night in France.....I sat still for a moment, engine running, and just moved the lever up and down the gearbox as you would do if you have just refilled it. I knew the gearbox was playing up a little but Mercedes assured me it was fine before I set off. Suddenly it got 'drive' and I drove to the tunnel with no issues. I got home OK too, but booked it straight in to a good auto box firm I know in the UK for an overhaul over Christmas. It has not missed a beat since.

CHAPTER 3

Silke Goes to England

My diary has much to say about our next trip...
(What? Didn't you think cats kept diaries?).

For some time now, the human had being saying
the word 'adventure' to me. I now know what this
is. Things arrive and are placed by the front door.
There is a new covered dirt box for me. Hmm.

There is a visit to Rosa. She does not prick me with
a needle, just checks me over. At home a suitcase
has been lying around for a week or so. The human
packs and re-packs it.
The car is parked in a new place and is heavily
loaded. Some of my personal things are in there
too.
In the morning the human puts my high level basket bed in too.

Then my human gets in the car with my harness,
he is not going without me. No way! So I run to get
in and we are off!

We are not going to the cattery, the car does not turn there, but to a big road with bright lights and barriers, so I sit in my high level basket and watch the world go by.

It rushes past. The human is driving very fast.

I go to the back shelf and the armrest and the basket.

Every so often the box woman on the windscreen starts talking, it sounds like she is angry.

I don't like her so I answer back with miaows. She can shut up.

My human puts on some music. I don't like it and miaow until he turns if off. That is better.

I love watching what happens at the toll barriers, we approach slowly, a thing goes bleep, lights change from red to green and the barrier goes up. The car speed rises, and off we go again, racing past the huge noisy trucks that do not seem so noisy in the car.

We stop to give the car a drink of some vile smelly stuff, then my human leaves me in the car with my lead tied onto the seat and he goes into a building. He comes back shortly and we move to a space away from the building, he lets me out, I cannot go far as the lead stops me. Then a huge truck grinds and grumbles and clatters its way past us before stopping, and, seeing me, produces huge hisses. I jump back in the car and crouch low so it can't see me. I don't like big trucks. This one is bigger than any I have seen. I see them everywhere here, this must be their home, on the big fast roads.

My human is eating and drinking some coffee. He wants me to eat and drink. I don't want to.

He gets back in the car and off we go. We have come a long way. After many more toll booths and many miles we stop again and the car gets its smelly drink. I still do not want to eat, drink or use the dirt box. Not when huge trucks come by scaring me.

All the noise and rush prevents me from sleeping properly but I just doze.
I am in my bed next to the human when we slow down in a queue of cars. I look on with interest as we stop, and slowly we inch forwards. There are officious looking men and women in blue uniforms and cars with flashing lights. They wave us through but some cars are pulled over and stopped.
The human says 'Welcome to France!'.

Every time that woman in the box on the windscreen speaks I yell at her to shut up. It is getting towards nightfall now, but my human and the car know where they are going, they don't need her to interrupt them.

We turn off the wide road and start going down some small roads. They are dark and turn and twist. I am tired and first get down onto the arm-rest then push my head onto the human's lap. Normally he does not let me come into his space in the car, but this time he does.

I snuggle; he says soft words and gives me a comforting little stroke. I love him.

We go through villages, I sit up and take notice but the car ignores my suggestions to stop. Then into dark countryside again.

Then we take a small turning and drive next to some big rocks, the road is not much bigger than the car. We come to a house and stop. Two kind humans are there to meet us.

Stuff is unloaded from the car. We go inside, and up to a room. At last the human takes off my harness and I can eat and use the dirt box.

I relax as he goes downstairs shutting me in the room. I can hear him downstairs, and I can hear a big dog.

He comes back later, I am so pleased to see him! We go to sleep snuggled up.

—-oooOOOooo—-

There is an alarm clock and it goes off. The human must have forgotten to turn it off. But it wakes the human up and he gives me breakfast, although it is still dark.

Then he goes downstairs for some breakfast of his

own. I want to come too, I can smell bacon! But he does not let me so I hiss at him.

When he comes up, he packs our things, then the kind lady and man come and she takes me on my harness and carries me downstairs.

We pass a HUGE dog behind a glass window door, but he can't get out, thank goodness.

Although it is still dark and cold the lady takes me for a little walk to a stream. I love it. I want to stay here for a while.

But then it is back into the car and we are off again, until a little further on we stop and we have a little walk with me on the harness.

Back in the car, the roads are slow at first as we wind through some mountains, then we get on the big fast roads again rushing past the big trucks.

We go though many tolls with their lights and barriers and we drive for hours and hours before we have to stop to give the car its smelly drink. It must be getting very tired by now.

The human gets some coffee and lets me out and takes me for a little walk. There are cats here! I want to say hello but they run away. My harness does not let me say hello. We walk around some grass, then get back into the car and drive for hours more. Every time I wake out of my doze the scenery is rushing by, we just don't stop.

We only stop to give the car a drink again. Greedy

thing. This time there are trucks everywhere and I am scared.

It is far into the night now. The car growls on relentlessly, I doze, in between telling the woman in the box to shut up. The human soothes me with a stroke every so often, but we just keep on going.

Finally we have slowed down and we come into a place with lots of lights. We stop at something that looks like a toll booth. The human talks to a woman inside it and she gives him a piece of paper which he attaches to the mirror, and we drive to another building.

He gets out, but then comes back and puts me in my carry box!

He takes me into the building; it is like going to the vet but it doesn't smell the same.

A gang of dogs is waiting in a queue before us. I yowl at them. I'm warning them. If they were not on leads or if I was on mine, there would be a fight.

A man waves a big plastic thing at me. My human says it is a scanner and not to worry, although what that is I have no idea.

Back in the car but out of my box, we have to queue with other cars then go through more narrow gaps with booths.

The people in them smile at me sitting in the front seat on my bed watching.

Then we stop at another barrier. The engine goes

off. I can smell the air. It is strange and my human grabs me puts me in my bed before he starts the engine and we go into a line of other cars before driving into a brightly lit narrow silver tunnel. The car gets waved at by a man who is telling it where to go, then the engine goes off and we sit.

An annoying loud voice outside makes me jump! 'Welcome to Le Shuttle train', he says, but then it goes all crackly and I can't understand what he is saying … I shout at the loud voice. Shut up!

Then, although the car is not started, there is a gentle motion and some rattles, I can see lights going by the windows then the windows go black and we are in a tunnel. The car is silent and the engine quiet. But we are moving!

The gentle motion is nice, it's soothing. My human and I are tired.

Then there is noise, doors opening, lights and engines starting, my human starts our engine and we are off out of the silver tunnel into the night.
The car has forgotten where we should be and is driving on the wrong side of the road!
But it seems everyone does it. In this strange place it must be allowed.

It starts to rain and the wipers come on, slip slop … I don't like it and think I might get wet so I go to the back shelf and stay there perfectly dry. The

rain rattles on the glass and the wipers slip slop ...
I sleep...

Eventually we go down some small dark roads, I come to the armrest and nuzzle my lovely human. We stop at a house and there is another man, he greets us and I go in on my lead which he holds while my human unloads the car.

The floors in this place are soft and furry and warm. I like this place.
It is smaller than my home in Spain, but cosy and warm.
This new man seems kind and gentle. My human gives me some food, shows me where my dirt box is, and we all go to bed very tired. What a long day! I sleep a lot.

In the morning, I meet another man who is also kind and gentle and a glamorous blonde woman. They all like me here. They play with me, stroke me and cuddle when I want to. This life is wonderful.

—-oooOOOooo—-

Next day I get to use the cat flap and learn that there is a garden here. It is lovely. Not big, not small. It has soft green grass, not like in Spain, and shrubs all around.

I can come and go at will. I love it. My human takes me to the front of the house and shows me a cat sized hole in a brick wall. After a cautious sniff I go through and it takes me behind a shed and into the garden. He meets me at the cat flap and tells me I am clever.

I love this place. It is meant for cats.

My human comes and goes, I am happy to catch up

on some sleep. I have no interest in going out in the car.

My human calls me, I go out of the front door with him, he calls me to follow him across the road, I follow, a little nervous. Then he goes into some woods. I follow. The smells are wonderful. Dead piles of leaves to rummage in. The earth smells different, the trees smell different. This place is heaven. I love it. We follow a path. Then he takes me into some woods to rummage around in. There is bracken. I like rummaging in that. There are birds singing, they make a lot of noise, there are squirrels high in the trees, too high for me to catch. What fun all this is!

Soon we go out like this every day. This is "walk" and he rattles his keys to tell me. I love it. One of the other men comes with us one day. I don't mind, there is plenty of room. I am quite relaxed and run and jump in the woods.

—-oooOOOooo—-

My human bundled me up out of my bed by the radiator and put the harness on me. I had been peacefully dozing most of the day.

He then took me out to the quiet blue car. I like this car. It smells wonderful 'Do you like the smell of leather?' the human says. I do, and its clean too.

He jumped into the seat with the wheel that was on the wrong side, and off we went.

At first I yowled at him. I mooched about. I did not want to go, I had had enough of cars for a while … but then, well, this was exciting, so I quietened down as the car quietly hummed along.

It is a very quiet smooth car.

We went onto a big fast road, and then after a short while onto some little roads through a small town.

Waiting for us, at a different house, were a family including some human kittens … I mean children.

They were all kind and gentle but the small ones were a little noisy for me at times.

They offered me some interesting new biscuits, and gently stroked me.

They all ate together and I sat on the sofa next to a brightly decorated tree that smelled faintly of plastic. Humans are odd, why did they have this plastic tree indoors?

All too soon on went the harness and we headed for home, just my forever human and me. Back the way we came. But not back to Spain.

—-oooOOOooo—-

I am beginning to understand that when humans go in cars, they often visit one another at their houses. Oh I know they go and get things too, and take me to the vet. But why are there times when they don't take me in the car?
Humans are curious sometimes.

My car, the big one we mostly travel in, came home today. It is large. A growling clattering gold coloured one with the big seats and box woman. Its engine makes a very distinctive sound. I know if we are going anywhere in *that* car, we might go on the long journey home to Spain.
But I don't want to get in it.
Not yet. I like it here in this curious country full of dead leaves, soft damp grass, birds and lovely woods.

—-oooOOOooo—-

NICE WALKS

The next day, my human made an attempt to take me for a walk but there were too many people around. I did not want to go. He tried again later when it was quieter and that was fine by me. We had a lovely time in the woods. I saw the squirrels again in the tops of trees and heard the big scary black birds flying around making "caw caw" noises.

My human led me on a different path on the way home, through some heather. I could smell the path had been used by an animal. I did not know what.

My human headed for the path to go home following a bigger path, but there was a smaller path I could follow. I reached the homeward path while he was still picking his way through the heather.

He lost sight of me and called me. I answered him back with a loud miaow. Then started walking back to get him, along the home path. He called, I miaowed, this was like rounding up kittens. He was pleased to see me and fussed me. I was happy to see him too. We got home just as it began to rain. What a lovely walk. I love my human.

—-oooOOOooo—-

Today the human made an early breakfast for me just as it was getting light. I love it when he does that.

When I had had breakfast, I sat looking out of the big glass window from the vantage point of the sofa, and some odd creature came into the pretty garden.
It had long ears, it hopped along slowly, and it had curious fluff for a tail.
It stopped and ate grass. I had never seen anything like it. It was nearly as big as me too.

I went quietly through the cat flap and with stealth went up the garden steps to get a better view of this odd creature.

It was time to have some fun.
I leapt up and raced at it, my killer cat instincts making me super alert, but never had I seen any-thing move so fast.
So clever too, jinking this way and that.
It did not go far and with one ear and and one eye it watched me while eating some more grass. I rushed again and again it moved so fast there was just air where it should have been.

Killer instinct switched off, now I knew this was

not going to be a meal. I was not hungry anyway.
But I decided I could still play chase with it.
It seemed to know what I was doing and knew that it could outrun me at any time.
Eventually it had enough and left the garden.
As my feet were now wet from the grass it was time for me to go back inside for a nap.

—-oooOOOooo—-

What an amazing country this is! So many different creatures, and birds singing everywhere. I am loving it.

It is Christmas time. Many houses have lovely lights twinkling. My forever human was going out in our car, the clattery long distance one, I leapt in. Where are we going?
He drove the short distance to the village and stopped outside a shop. The village sparkled with Christmas lights and even the trees had lights on them.

He went into a very smelly shop. I waited in the car and watched the twinkling lights. After a while he came out with smelly food. Fish and chips! I don't think I like fish.

He offered me a small piece of the soft white fish.
No thank you, very kind of you to offer.

The following day, we got in my usual car, the quiet smooth blue one had disappeared, and we drove a little further than we would go in the blue car, but not much.

My human put on my harness when we stopped and put me in the cat carry basket. I had noticed he had also put my dirt box in the car.

When we stopped another human came to help carry stuff from the car into a large building.

We went upstairs into an apartment.
We spent Christmas day there. It is a special day for
humans although all they did was ate and chatted. I dozed on the sofa amongst them. The rain splashed down outside and I went on the balcony, but we were up high with no way down for me to

escape.

When the evening came, I wanted to go home I scratched at my cat carrier, my human heard me. He understood me! Very soon he said his farewells, and we were in the car going home.

I was out of my carrier in the car. We drove on the big fast road back to the house.

—-oooOOOooo—-

The next day I took the human on a longer different walk down a path I had wanted to explore before.

We had to cross a small road and go along a wide and open path by a lake.

A man came running fast the other way and I bolted for home.

My human called me and came to find me. I came reluctantly at first. I know I must trust him but I did not like the running man and hoped he would not come back

I stopped to yowl at the ducks floating on the pond. That made me forget about the running man. Then I ran to catch up to my human.

Later we went into the woods on a wide path. I liked this. We crossed the little road and stopped by a bench. I knew this bench. The path home was nearby as well as my favourite bracken woods.

My human barged through the bushes on a small track into the woods and made for a wide path for our walk. I dawdled in the bushes. I smelled cat.

I came out into the clearing and a fine cat trotted majestically towards me.
He was white with tabby bits. He was really calm, not making a fuss. He came to a stop nearby and just stood, without any threat, so best to look at me.

I thought he was very handsome.

I walked after my human and stopped to look back. The attractive cat was following us.

We walked a little further. We stopped. He stopped. I did a frisky four leg jump and galloped behind a tree going down on the ground ready for a playful pounce.
He walked up to me slowly and deliberately. I shot off in another jump and gallop, tail up, and hid under some bracken.

This English gentleman cat is just so elegant I thought.

I trotted along after my human. Gentleman cat came too. I stopped to check often.

Then, when we were near the end of the walk, he veered off into the bracken.

The next morning, I trotted along eagerly to see if he would be there waiting for me. He was!

My human barged through the brambly bushes and walked ahead to sit on a log and watch.

When I was sure he could see me, I jumped and galloped and crouched down to play.
Gentleman cat followed but no play.

This cat was so sophisticated; and so handsome.

He came towards me slowly and touched my nose with his. I shot into the air and galloped off behind a tree.
He quietly came up and round the the side I was not watching. So I jumped and galloped away again.

This game was such fun!

This continued throughout our walk until once more he veered off into the bracken going a different way home.

What a fabulous Gentleman Cat.

The third morning I led my human determinedly to the woods to find the Gentleman Cat. We got through the bushes into the clearing but he was not there.

At first I was disappointed then, as time went on and he still did not appear, I got sad. My human looked around for him but he was nowhere to be seen.

I sat in the clearing. I did not want to go anywhere.

Where was Gentleman cat?

My human sat on a log and waited too.

After a long time he called me and started to walk off. Reluctantly I followed, looking over my shoulder for this English Gentleman cat.

Never had I met such well mannered cat. Did I mention that he was so handsome too.

I sat down, feeling sad and rejected.

My human seemed to know this. He sat near me on a tree stump. Then came and picked me up giving me a hug while we walked on through the woods.

I never saw Gentleman Cat again, as the next day we set off to Spain ... sometimes I still dream of being romanced by him once more.

—-oooOOOooo—-

Back at the house, he packed things into the car, including my special high-level bed. I knew we were going to travel again and I carefully explored the garden. I wanted to remember how nice this place was. I knew we were leaving, but I wanted to come back.

We headed for the big fast road, today it was still

full of big trucks. It was daylight so lots for me to see. The countryside was dead looking but I knew it would be spring soon and it was nearly ready to burst into life.

We stopped at a big parking place. Then we drove to a toll booth, the man inside looked at my little book which my human handed to him.
The window was down but I could not get out as I was on my harness.
"Look everyone this guy has a cat with him!" he said, and then, rather cheekily he ruffled the fur on my head!

He handed the book back to my human and we drove quietly to a long queue of cars.
There with the engine off people and cars crowded round us, I yelled and yowled.
"Come on, lets get going!" I shouted.

Then some men got angry with an important looking lady in a bright jacket. Announcements yelled at us, I yelled back. We sat for ages. Then suddenly my human got into action, started the car and we drove off slowly in a queue of cars only to stop, engine off again not very far on.
It took a while longer, but at last, we once more drove onto LeShuttle ... the tunnel that moves.

It was night when we got to an hotel. The box woman had been talking again and I was fed up with shouting... Why didn't she get the message and shut up!

We went up to a nice warm room and while my human went downstairs for dinner and I sat on the windowsill watching cars on a road nearby and some twinkling lights. I was quite used to staying in different places now. It was all very interesting.

I was in a playful mood. The human is feeling the cold a little now so pulled up that big squashy thing that is so nice to snuggle in on the bed. I like it so I decided to have a game with him.

We cats like to pat without extending our claws and gently nip when we want to play. It's a handy way to get attention and, if the human does not respond in a reasonable time and play, it is a simple matter to nip a little harder or scratch if he still won't co-operate.

He was up for it quickly enough though and soon got the message and we had a jolly play fight.

The human tried to put me down before I was ready, though, so I gave him a hug and climbed onto his neck so he got the message and we played a little more.

Then I got bored and jumped down to go out, but of course the human had closed the door!
That made me cross so I got back on the snuggly thing and gave him a 'death hug' and a nip!

Good night, human. we can play again tomorrow.

—-oooOOOooo—-

In the morning we got back in the car and drove again. Around lunchtime we stopped at a nice wooded area and the human took me for a walk on my lead. I liked it.
Then from nowhere a dog came rushing at me. It was a shock so, without thinking. I went up a tree. Dogs can't climb trees.

Humans came to catch the dog. I growled at my human for plucking me off the tree before I could get high up it. I struggled but he gripped me tighter on his shoulder and walked towards our car. We were nearly there when the dog got loose again and charged towards us. I growled, but I was nearly as safe on the human's shoulder as up that tree. Stupid dog!

The humans came and got the dog, cross with it. We got in the car and started to drive again.

Finally we came off the big fast road and onto smaller ones. A little while later we arrived at the nice place with the big dog and lovely humans. I knew the humans would keep the dog away, and unlike my last encounter with one of his species, he seemed a genial soul, much less likely to cause me any problems.

We settled in. I knew this room and now I knew we were going home to Spain. I was happy.

It was a cold night and I snuggled next to my human on the squashy thing, sharing warmth. I love him.

In the morning we set off again, along some small roads this time.
We stopped and had a walk in some trees and bushes. Very nice.
Back in the car, we got on a big fast road, with so many trucks around. I had never seen so many.

We got to a toll and got stuck in traffic. The engine went off and I yelled, "come on move, get on with it!"
Then the other cars and trucks got angry hooting their horns and yelling. I yelled too, but nothing

happened.

Cars and big trucks all around, people out of their cars. We waited for ages, but my human was quiet and calm. I just wanted to go and get away from all this noise.
Then horns from the big trucks started making a fearsome angry noise. What ever was the matter? Why couldn't we go?

Then suddenly the human started the engine, and we inched forwards, cars all around us pushing into the lanes and being squeezed from a wide, wide road down to two rows side by side. I hated the big trucks being next to us especially one that rattled and got much too close. They kept hissing too although it can't have been at me because by then I was hiding.
I didn't like this.

At last we were free to drive on.

Ages later we went through another toll area with no one around.

I sensed soon that the smells of the earth were different and familiar. We were nearer home. We were in Spain!

It was such a relief I fell into a deep sleep on my back with my paws up. I was happy. I was safe. I was nearly home!

I dreamt of the things I had seen, and places I had been. What an adventure we have had!

We got home in the evening. I stood at the dash-board as we went along the little lanes near home. I could see the mountain! I mewed at the human 'I know where I am now!'.

When the engine went off, the human opened the door and took off my harness.
I jumped out and stretched and started to inspect the place as he unloaded the car.

I smell cat! I pee to let them know I'm back. This is still my territory!

I am home, with the hard rich red earth, the plants I know. The house I know so well.

What an adventure! I love my forever human and he loves me.
Now I know where he went when he left me at the cat hotel. Next time he is *not* going to do that. I won't let him.

I will go in his suitcase, if I have to. We will not be parted again. I am a travelling cat and I am very special.

My forever human is special too. He is mine. Forever.

AND RELAX …

Silke was once again very aware of her surroundings on our travels, but funnily enough she really got alert as we crossed the Spanish border on the way back and then relaxed with a complete paws up moment in her

basket. That was quite comical and shows how safe she felt.

CHAPTER 4

A walk on the wild side

I tried walking Silke regularly on her lead some time before we attempted a long journey.

There are some woods nearby that are a popular dog walk and of course wild boar lurk there too. I had seen their hoof prints in the mud many times.

Silke loves these woods and now, some years later she actually walks there off the lead.

On the first occasion there was one bush she was far too interested in. I am always nervous in case she flushes out a boar! Worse a defensive wild boar mother and piglets.
We have a route like a figure eight and Silke usually jumps into the car at the end as she knows that is time to go home.

Around that time, when visiting the vet, I tried walking Silke into the surgery on her lead. Rosa's chin hit the floor and everyone in the building stared, stunned into silent wonder.

All the dog owners and young vets could not believe it. Cat owners with their charges in boxes were dumbfounded that Silke was just on a lead.
Rosa says Silke is the only cat who does this.
She sits on a chair next to me or on my knee if its busy. Dogs that come too close get hissed and cuffed at.

After the surgery visit is over, she has to come into the office where I pay, she does not want to do this and generally just wants to leave immediately.
But then, when its time to go she trots determinedly to the exit door and once outside loiters, while she makes her mind up if she will come to the car or wants to go exploring.

Of course, if she trots obediently to the car and jumps in people in the veterinary surgery looking on start chattering … Even if I have assisted her into the car as she stands at the dash board when we drive off, they are amazed.

I understand we have achieved a certain celebrity status and people in the town know all about the old man that drives around with his cat on the loose in his car. I'm told they look out for us.

—-oooOOOooo—-

INVADERS!

I live with a kind human. I love him, he loves me back. I always like to know where he is, and I am never far away from him.

I may have mentioned that we live in a nice spacious house in Spain. I have a cat flap in a door and can come and go as I wish. It lets me into a little courtyard. I have had the human add some shelves that run up a wall and I can use these to go over into the garden. I love this!

My human feeds me every day both wet and dry food, but what food I don't eat he puts out in the garden for the wild cats! I do NOT approve!
They may look like ordinary house cats but they are wild. They will attack humans if they are cornered and scared and just want to run away. And they are always hungry.

I don't like the wild cats in my garden. They feed and go. I will not let them stay here. It is my space. My territory.

One in particular annoys me. He is a big striped

tabby cat and is a local bully boy. He yowls at my human demanding food night and day.

My human has many people who come to see him. They all like me and they make a lot of happy human noise. I watch and doze. Happy humans are nice, but wild cats are not!

Once a small young grey cat, barely more than a kitten, came to drink from the pool. I could see she was hungry and thirsty. She was painfully thin so I was prepared to allow her a drink.

But then bully cat came out from the bushes, running at her from behind, and roughed her up. Poor little grey cat!

I am not having that, I thought, so I leaped from my vantage point on a handy patio chair and charged at the bully, swearing and screaming. Hearing all the noise, my human dashed out of the house and the bully ran off scared.

The little grey cat ran off too, but she was unharmed.

The human fussed me and I know I did the right thing. That sort of behaviour on my personal territory will not be tolerated!

DEALING WITH SILKE'S UNINVITED GUESTS

Cats are fiercely territorial, it is a reflection of their primeval nature to protect their hunting areas.

Silke frequently has a 'yowl off' with another cat.

At my villa, when I first moved in I felt sorry for two tabby feral cats, who I later came to know as Laurel and Hardy. I would give them some biscuits, and whatever food Silke had left, sometimes topping it up with some cheap stuff.

Of course they were there before Silke. That stopped her not one bit from taking them on.

Laurel got it first and accorded Silke respect from then on. But Hardy was different, a large tough tabby street cat who stood his ground. Laurel was so called because he kinked his tail in such a way that you could be thinking you were looking at Stan Laurel scratching his head at times.

Hardy the big tough guy with a mean streak, well that suited him too.

Even when I caught Hardy and had him neutered he was still tough. Hardy lives on today, Laurel has disappeared. They were friendly towards each other so must have been related in some way.

The food I put down attracted many other feral cats. Including a gorgeous grey barely grown up kitten that was bullied without mercy by the others.

She was so hungry and desperate I even took to trying to feed her separately. One day this little cat had managed a feed and was taking a drink from the pool.

Hardy did not like that at all and dashed up to the poor little thing and roughed her up.

A streak of black lightning shot into action as Silke rammed hard into Hardy without warning. He was so surprised he trotted off a short distance to take stock of what had hit him.

The little one had bolted and was rarely seen again. I was outside and walking towards Silke to make sure she did not get hurt, as I approached she charged at Hardy again but with me coming towards him as well he bolted which told Silke all she needed to know and she chased him off though the hedge.

Perhaps protecting the little one was her massive ma-

ternal instinct coming into play. I have never seen another cat do this for a stranger.

If I show Silke videos on my laptop of kittens she takes great interest.

I have always expected her to bring home a bedraggled kitten from somewhere!

—-oooOOOooo—-

On one occasion I was driving off from the house and went a different route, past where a number of feral cats make their homes in a barranca, which is a reed filled storm drainage channel, mostly dry but when in flood is full of dangerous fast moving rain water coming off the nearby mountain.

This is where I think the little grey cat came from. A man was getting cages out of a white van. I stopped and said hello and told him about the little grey cat and the big tabby.

He was German and spoke good English. He said "Really? I have been after that big tabby for ages." Cats normally have a well defined territory so the barranca must have been his territory.

I asked how the traps worked and offered to let him put one in the garden to see if it would catch Hardy.

I told him we must be careful not to catch my neighbour's cats. "No problem," he said "If we do we will just let them out if you know what they look like. I don't suppose they are chipped are they?" he said.

Then he showed me how the trap worked, with its pressure plate and a door that closes and has a very easily tripped spring.

As agreed, that evening he came round and dropped off a trap. We set it up in the front drive in a corner Hardy makes his own by peeing everywhere.

Sure enough, in the morning there he was banging around in the trap, jumping off the sides, very scared.

I messaged the German and he told me to put a towel over the cage that would calm him down. It worked like a charm. The effect was instantaneous.

Silke was of course very interested; sniffing and peeping under the towel to see who was there.

He came round and transferred Hardy into a travel cage with a sliding side to contain him if he was violent. Which he most certainly was.

In the evening he brought Hardy back. Gingerly we opened the door to the cage, and he bolted, even though he was still a little unsteady on his feet.
It was quite obvious that he knew exactly where he was too as he shot through the front gate and into a neighbour's villa, which backs onto the barranca.

Of course he'd peed in the cage and Silke had a good sniff of that, pulling her 'stinky face' afterwards. This is where she will have her mouth open, form a grimace, and move her head around to literally taste the smell. All cats do this.

The German man said "Got any more you would like to catch?" I thanked him and a made a cash contribution to Hardy's missing balls.

He'll be much more friendly in six weeks or once the testosterone has worked out of him.

---oooOOOooo---

CHAPTER 5

Silke does construction

Pedro is a builder. He likes me. I like him.

Pedro and his troop of men come and start work on the house. It is loud and noisy. Mostly they work outside.

I watch what they are doing carefully. They dig holes, build walls and make horrible noises with machines.

They start early, and finish late with a siesta in the middle of the day, and a break at 10.00 in the morning. That is when they feed me ham.
I like ham, not that fancy stuff, mind. Just sandwich ham. They have coffee, eat sandwiches and laugh together. Sometimes they play fight with me. I don't use my claws and only nip them with my teeth. I like to be with the men.

I particularly love watching the bricklayers. Especially old Diego. He stinks of the cigarettes he smokes.

He takes some of that mud that goes hard, slops it onto a brick and then lays a new brick on top with more mud that goes hard, then he taps it to exactly where he wants it to be.

After a while he has built a whole wall, and the next day I can see that the mud that goes hard is like rock. I love watching him at work. Humans are quite clever with their hands sometimes. Diego is a kind old man.

It gets hotter everyday, the summer is coming, I remember this time last year. My last life (have I mentioned that cats have nine lives?) was far less pleasant, but now I am in this lovely place with my human and the builders.

I greet my human when he comes home even if it is late at night and I am tired from helping the builders all day. I jump in the car and drive with him into the driveway and show him what the builders have done today.

Big machines come and move earth. They are noisy and scary. But when they are not working I climb over them. They are quiet, and peaceful after a hard day of work. They smell of dust and earth and that foul stuff they drink.

I love Pedro, he is top cat and the builder humans do what he tells them. Digging, drilling, cutting, mixing, moving things around. They are very busy. The house my human and I live in is changing ever so slowly but surely.

Human visitors come and look around, so I go to show them what has been done that day. I know what happened because I watched them do it!
They like to see what has been done in the day and inspect the work.

The workmen call me La Jeffa, The Boss.
I like to know what is happening. Sometimes I walk on the mud that goes hard when it is still soft, leaving paw prints. But I don't like that stuff on my paws, it tastes nasty too and sticks in my toes. It takes ages for me to lick it off. It smells when its wet so I learn to leave it alone.

I love exploring all the new things, especially the new holes, and strange underground places with water in them. The machines dig so deep, so fast.

There are big trucks coming too, some with long arms lifting loads of bricks over the walls, some dumping mounds of sand, or gravel.
I hide from them, I don't like them. They are noisy and scary. They hiss at me sometimes when they stop, so I keep away.

Sometimes the human sets me on a wall out of the way to watch them. I usually tell him off, growling at him. I'm in charge here! I am La Jeffa!

---oooOOOooo---

Oh the joy of a dust bath! My human chuckles at me, he says I am now a white cat with a black face as I find some lovely white sand to roll in!

I like to use the sand for a toilet. The builders are not so keen when they mix the sand and find a smelly lumpy bit!

My human swims in the pool! I wish he would not. I don't like splashes so keep well away.

I like how the house and garden is changing, it all feels safer. There are places to sit and be quiet.

To start with they just seemed to be knocking things down and pulling things out, but now they seem to be bringing in new things and making it nicer. They even took bits of the roof off and put it back on again in a different place. I have no idea why, but I'm sure the human likes it.

There is even a separate house for some of the cars to live in, and an enormous hole underneath it with more rooms for me to explore.

I am not sure of the air conditioning. The house can get cold. I no longer sleep on my human's bed. It is too cold. I don't like the cold air blowing at me.

Cats like sleeping in warm places. I love finding a shady spot in the bushes and sleep outside in the daytime or in another room if it is night time. I have many places to choose from.

For a long time I couldn't drink from the pool.

Pedro and his men let all the water out of it and then started pulling the shiny things off the sides and spoiling it.

I didn't like that. But eventually they stuck new shiny bits where the old ones came off and filled it up again, so I decided to forgive them.

Many visitors came, new people all the time, they like my human, and they get happy and noisy together.

The builders worked relentlessly through the summer. Gates move, walls move, machines come and go. Pedro fusses me. So do the men. I like them all. They are my men. I inspect their work.

I am La Jeffa, Spanish for the boss. I have to know what is going on. I watch them all the time. Until it is time for my sleep.

—-oooOOOooo—-

Every morning, when my men arrive, my human makes them coffee. He unlocks the gates and drives the cars out of the way. I often ride in the cars. He then has his breakfast while tapping and tapping at his computer.

I come to the window to make him open it and let me in. I have a cat flap but it is nice to make my human let me in. Sometimes we do this more than once. It is my game with him.

My human got out a suitcase! I don't like this.
Then he is gone. Now I only have the builders for company.
At first I am worried about food, but the food still comes. Pedro feeds me. So do some other gentle friends of my human. They smell faintly of cat.

They are good people. But I miss my forever human. The cars are still here. Quietly sitting. Underneath they are cold when they do not run and go places. When is my human coming back? Where has he gone?!

One warm afternoon I am snoozing in Pedro's van. He jumps in and we go to his house. I am quiet, enjoying the journey. It is good to be travelling again. When we get there I miaow and he is shocked to see me, but instead of inviting me in, he drives me straight back to my house without stopping.
It is not the same as being driven by my human.

Pedro's children come round to play, one is very little, one is bigger. They love playing. I have to learn their games. They have to learn mine!

All the men are now aware that I like to play hide

and pounce, grabbing their ankles and nipping them! Then I gallop off so they can't catch me! We play this all the time.

The children swim in the pool! They are getting all wet but they are making happy noises. I call to Pedro to stop them getting wet, but he just laughs.

My human is gone. I notice that he is not here mostly at night when the house is quiet and the builders have gone. I am lonely.
When the men do not come, on the day they call Sunday, I am all alone.
Where, oh where, is my forever human? Has he deserted me? I cry for him in the night, but he doesn't come.

But then suddenly my forever human is back! I race to see him! We fuss. I am so happy!
'Did you miss me?' he says, but I have my pride, so I do not answer.

He empties his suitcase and puts it away. I am happy. Everyday we fuss now. I love him so much. I rush to meet him whenever he comes home. I rush to try and get in the car whenever he leaves. I want to come ... don't leave me behind again!

—-oooOOOooo—-

He takes me on longer and longer journeys. He thinks I like one particular car. No; I just want to be with him. I don't care about the car, even if it is the slow noisy old one.

At night we go to some big and very fast roads. We go fast too. There are strange lights, noises, and barriers that go up, then we go really fast, and pass the big trucks like they are standing still.

I like to sit on the armrest with my human and reach out a paw for reassurance as he drives. Especially when we go through the tolls with their big red and green lights and barriers that lift up out of our way.

I like to sit on the wide back shelf too. I can see out and see the world rush by. The trucks can't catch us!

—-oooOOOooo—-

THINGS SETTLE DOWN

It is high summer. The builders do quiet jobs like painting inside as they are not allowed to make noise. The paint stinks. Then after a few days it stops stinking. I'm glad.

It is hot. Insects are around that sting. I itch.

The human does not like the dust that comes from the work. I do not like my food when it is covered in dust. But we like that it is quiet.

But the machines come back and dig an even bigger deeper hole in the garden. It is very noisy again.

Big trucks come too to take rock and dirt away. Noise everywhere. This hole is so big I do not want to go into it. Even the humans use a ladder to go down into it. Piles of earth are everywhere.

It is time for the big rains and they start very heavily. The rich red earth gets hard to dig as it is soft but heavy. So I use the sand heaps even more for my toilet! The builders are used to this and when they find my smelly poo they say "Oh, Silke!"

There are new men now doing different jobs. Men with shiny pipes and snaky wires. The main crew are still here with Pedro. They are nice men and all of them like me. I am La Jeffa.

I like to watch them all. They move dirt around. They make the mud that goes hard in different colours. One is white and they cover the walls with it.

There is so much for me to inspect! I must know exactly what is happening on my territory! This is important cat stuff!

The wild stripy bully cat sits on top of the biggest pile of earth. It is his look out. I don't like him up there. I growl at him.

A fierce rain storm suddenly comes with a lot of rain and wind. I am up on the roof! I cower under the tiles behind a small wall. I can hear my human calling me, he is worried and I am not surprised.

But I am not moving! Not till this horrible storm passes.

One side of me is already all wet where the roof doesn't cover me. I don't want my other side to be wet as well! Cats do not like to be wet!

Finally the storm calms down, and I run to my human who has been calling and calling me.
A sharp wind catches me and I have to use my tail to balance, it goes round in circles as I run across the wall.

My human is there to fuss me. He tells me off gently, saying that I am a silly cat for being out in this weather. I'm not a silly cat! Only half of me got wet, after all!

I lick my wet fur to make it dry and curl up safe and sound in the house listening to the storm outside.

The builders can't work when it is like this but the storm is still making a noise. Noise everywhere, disturbing a cat's sleep.

—-oooOOOooo—-

CHAPTER 6

Silke's big summer adventure

If I want to go in the car, I go straight to the back shelf, because my human finds it harder to get me out if he does not want me to go. Ha Ha!

Sometimes my human takes me to the smelly shop for hot fish and chips. Although it seems unnatural as fish are cold, I try a little bit of the hot white fish. I like it! He shares some with me. I now like this fish, although not too hot. I want my share when he brings that home!

Fish are quite a versatile food, it seems. One day he made kippers. I liked that a lot.

The spring has come and we have several different sets of visitors. I like them all.

My human has been taking me to a cafe in my harness. I behave and wait while he has a coffee. But on one occasion I needed the toilet.

As far as I can see, the nearest earth is in a pot with a plant in it, just beside our table. I dig and do my business.

There is dirt around the pot where I have dug it out. Nice soft dirt, just right for a cat.

But my human is upset. It seems this is not supposed to be a cat toilet.

My human says sorry to the cafe owner who comes out with a dustpan and clears the dirt back into the pot. What a fuss!

—-oooOOOooo—-

A SLIP UP
AMONGST THE
POT PLANTS

Sometimes, if we have to visit the vet, we go to the cafe next door, and I'm surprised they still let us in … because this is where Silke revealed her attitude to pot plants.

Normally she would sit beautifully, while I have a cup of coffee, and observe the goings-on with interest.

On this occasion she was under the table on the floor and I could not immediately see what she was up to.

It seems she decided she needed the toilet, and to her the pot plants, with their nice soft earth, were just what she was looking for.

She threw dirt everywhere while doing her business. And no, you cannot stop her without a heck of a fight as she does not understand why these are not excep-

tionally fine toilets, with nice soft earth, placed there just for her personal use!

NEW PLACES

My human goes away for a weekend, but it is OK, a nice lady called Isabel and her human kitten Javier come to stay. I like Javier he is a nice quiet and gentle human kitten. I cuddled up to him and let him stroke me.

Pedro has two human kittens. Rico is OK. Ángel is not, he is rough with me and throws stones. I do not trust him and yowl at him to leave me alone.

We have a party with many people at the house. Too many people for me. Some I know, many I don't. So I am grumpy.

Then, when my human comes back, three ladies come to stay. They are loud and funny and lovely. Two have come before. They all love my human. They all stay up late, drinking wine and laughing. It is good to have them around and my human is happy.
So am I! I have several different beds to choose for night time snuggles!

Then out comes my human's suitcase again. He starts to pack. I sleep on his clothes. He is not going anywhere without me!

He takes me to see Rosa and gives her the special little book that is all about me. It is called a passport and Rosa makes a mark in it. I am nice to Rosa today, I am on her territory in her office, after all.

In the evening we all get in the quiet blue car and go to a restaurant by the sea. We sit at a table on a balcony. The owner will not let me sit on a seat but the floor is OK. I am happy. I watch the sea from a safe distance. I like watching the bubbles and waves in the water. The sea smells and its wet, but it is where the fish live so it is interesting to a cat.

When it is time to go, of course I am on my lead and harness.

People in the restaurant point and stop talking to watch me steering my human on the lead.
I don't care, this is fun for me to explore.

In the car park there are stray cats, they are very interested in me. I am not interested in them *at all*, I want to go home.
They can see I am on a lead. One wants to sniff my bottom!
I snap round and bash him with a hiss. He soon leaves me alone.

I am a Princess. They are uncouth street cats! How dare they approach me!

I am a travelling cat and we are going on an adventure!

—-oooOOOooo—-

CHAPTER 7

Preparations

*M*y *travelling companions consisted of two American ladies and one Canadian, and a Bahamian gentleman.*

We travelled in two cars; the red Mustang and the Mercedes.
Brian drove the Mercedes and said afterwards, "Man! I never drove so far and so fast in my life! I'm used to driving in Nassau in the Bahamas where the speed limit is mostly under 30 m.p.h. and New Providence Island is only twenty miles long and ten miles wide!".
Bless him, motorway speeds seemed daunting to him at first.
The set up was that one lady took it in turns to travel with Silke and I, and two ladies travelled with Brian.
We headed north to one of my grotty reps special hotels near Le Mans.

There an was instant revolt when we arrived though, and it was not good enough for my guests. So we headed off into Calavdos country to one they con-

sidered better.

Well, I concede that it was; apart from the agonising wait for dinner as a coach party had arrived and we were in second place to them.
No doubt chaos reigned supreme in the kitchen.

Before dinner it was time to stretch Silke's legs a bit, so we went for a walk around the car park and then to a small lake in the garden. But to get back into the hotel we had to cross a driveway with an enormous coach disgorging passengers.
Silke wanted to bolt.
Big coaches to her are as scary as big trucks.

I picked her up and held on tight, and got us through the electric sliding doors, which were not her favourite thing either, so that I could set her down and take her to our room.

It was a nice room on the ground floor, but on the other side of the window the coach was parked up. Silke was rigid with fear until the driver turned off its engine, then she realised it was staying out there and not coming into the room!

Now the great thing with Silke is, once she is in the room with dirt box and food, she will settle down. She will quietly doze the evening away until I come back. When I come back though she is of course loose in the room, so you have to be careful she does not bolt out of the door. Hotels usually have fire doors that prevent her going far, but you never know.

After a comfortable night and breakfast we set off again.

For the Channel Tunnel, you can pay extra to pick a time and then be put on the next train once you get there. The system is called 'Flexi-plus'.
This is how I had booked our group's tickets. This was peak holiday season after all.

So we arrived mob handed at the pet centre with two cars and already late as, following the Calvados country diversion, my journey was now out of kilter, so Silke and I faced quite a delay in the pet centre which was very busy.

Once through that, with tickets and passes hanging off the mirror, we headed for the ticket booth. But there was no possibility of traveling around seven or eight lanes of solid traffic to get to the Flexi-plus lane.
Once at the booth, consternation from the officials, but at least some understanding of our position broke out.

They realised we were travelling together, and we were directed to queue jump the traffic.

The filthy looks we got from those queuing was a little unsettling. One angry guy was even made to go backwards because he tried to cut us off.
The French officials were having none of that.

The same happened at passport control. A space for us was forced upon the hapless motorists, and we went to the head of the queue.

The Americans were mighty impressed!

Off we went and without a queue; and were immediately waved onto a train and parked inside. Again our colonial visitors were impressed...

'What the hell happened there? Have we got diplomatic immunity or something?'

We laughed and joked about it all and Silke, perhaps assuming this was just the treatment which should be accorded to a cat like her, was good as gold.

—-oooOOOooo—-

A HAPPY BAND
OF TRAVELLERS

Something is going on. No late night laughing and drinking on the terrace. It is an early night for everyone.

In the morning, my human packs the Mustang with my things, his things and things from the ladies. Meantime the tired man, now rested from his awful flight, packs my usual car.

We must be going on an adventure again. I am excited and inspect what they are doing. My travel box is on the back seat in the Mustang. I'm going with my human and one of the ladies. I know we are going a long way too.

The journey is the one I know, with toll barriers, I miaow when the little box squeaks in the car and the barrier goes up. But at least there is no box woman in this car.

We have to make stops for coffee too. Humans can't seem to go for too long without coffee.

The big trucks sound louder in this car with its squashy fold down convertible roof, but my box is in the back and it is cosy and dark so I feel safe and hidden. It is nice to have the lady in the car and listen to her and my human talking.

I come forward and visit them every so often and nuzzle the lady. She says she is amazed at how happy I am travelling in the car. But this is old stuff for me ... I am a travelling cat!

It is hot outside and although the car blows cold air at us, I am happy because it stops us getting too hot.

We are taking a different route this time. We travel on smaller roads climbing into the mountains. The scenery is beautiful and I notice the air changing, its so fresh. I like it.

We stop for coffee yet again and the cars have their smelly drink. My human lets me have a little walk around the car park, but I am scared when a posse of noisy motorcycles arrives. I get back in the car and hide in my box.

I am about to get out of the car after the motorbikes have gone, when a huge truck stops and hisses at me. I scurry back into the car and hide in the box. It is my sanctuary cave. I don't like big trucks, and it seems they don't like me.

When we drive off I am happy. I come out of

the box. My human says we are going higher into something called the Pyrenees.

We are coming into a town called Puigcerda. My human can read the signs, he doesn't need box woman to tell us where we are.

The scenery is nice. I would like to stop and explore but we drive on. I stay awake to watch the dramatic scenery pass by. I look over the lady's shoulder for the best view.

We have been climbing and climbing and climbing, higher and higher into the mountains but finally, beyond another little town high in the Pyrenees, we start to go down again. The road twists and turns and sometimes there is a stream rushing along beside the road.

My human opens the windows just enough for me to put my nose out, and I smell the beautiful air with all its interesting smells. I hear the noise of the stream tumbling along beside the road, and the car follows the twisting road, left corner, right corner, left corner, right corner.

The road is very twisty so we do not go fast. On and on it goes.

The lady loves it and is constantly saying 'Oooh and Aaah' which usually, in human speak, means there is something that they are excited about. I listen. I smell. I love.

We go through another small village and then onto a bigger road....it looks familiar to me. Then we turn onto the little road that takes us to see the nice man, the lady and Athos the great big dog. I have been here before!

Athos comes out, excited to see us arrive, barking and limping, and anxious to stick his nose in the car, I hiss and jump on the roof where he cannot get me.
I learned later that Athos likes cats, but to me, as we arrive, he is big, scary, noisy and rambunctious.
Poor Athos; he limps because he is old so he cannot run and jump as he once did. As dogs go, I quite like Athos.

The man and the nice lady help unload the cars. They seem pleased to see us and there is a smell of cooking in the house. I am hungry.
It is nice to be back here in the same room as before, I am happy.
I can hear the humans laughing and having dinner downstairs.

My human comes to bed, and just as we are about to go to sleep there is a lot of excited shouting.

We rush to the window and my human puts me on the window cill.
Now I can see why. I can see them. I growl.
Wild boar are out in the field next door feeding. I

hope they can't get in here.

When they go away it gets darker and we sleep. It is warm so I do not have to snuggle.

—-oooOOOooo—-

THE WILDLIFE PUTS IN AN APPEARANCE

We returned that summer to Hotel La Folie and I had a splendid evening meal with my American friends while Silke stayed happily upstairs.

It was from the window of this room that she saw the pine marten, which is a dog sized ferret, and some wild boar.

She was hissing out of the window and growling. She saw the wild boar crossing the horse paddock, unconcerned on their evening rummage.

The next day it was off to La Rochelle, not so far in the scheme of things; a little North of Bordeaux.
I love La Rochelle and have found an excellent hotel there. This though was to be Silke's first experience of lifts. She does not like them at all.

However, once the dirt box and food are installed, she

can be left to peacefully sleep in the hotel room so we all went off for a jolly meal, then a wander around La Rochelle.

The next day, I dispatched my friends for a day on their own and a wander about, while Silke and I made for the local park, which appeared large with canals running through it.

First we had to do battle with the lift. When the doors opened Silke performed a series of huge leaps to get out of it, thankfully restrained by the lead.

Then we had the revolving door, which led onto the street and almost immediately a large bus racing around a corner made Silke to just want to run as fast as she could anywhere.

We turned a corner not going to the park but towards boatyards, and as we got there and she started to relax, a circular saw started up!

She was terrified. I put her on my shoulder, held her tight and set off to the park.

It was not far and as I set her down on the ground and we followed a path next to a canal, she visibly relaxed.

She was on the lead but I did not trust her not to bolt, not knowing what she would see or meet.

We ambled along the path in the shade of some ill kept woods. A jogger came by and I put Silke in a tree which she was happy about. Especially when another followed with a dog.

Then we came to a bridge that would allow us access

to the green lawns of the park on the other side of the canal and some peacocks crying a little further on.

It was a road bridge and I watched a bus cross it. With no other option, I picked up Silke, holding her tightly, and crossed quickly.

We walked along a little way and sat on a bench for a while, then looped back around to the canal making towards the road bridge.
Then I saw potential trouble in the form of a horse drawn tourist carriage coming across the bridge to our side.
It stopped, dropped off its tourists and the horses were rested standing in the shade. Fortunately they were quiet.

I wanted to go under the bridge on the canal path but Silke shied away from that.
The horses had by now moved off so I picked Silke up and crossed the road.
I set her down, just as she spotted the horses coming along at a trot pulling their wagon.

She bolted and fought with the harness, but I went with her and she hid in a clump of grass watching the horses go by.
She stayed there for a few moments calming down, and I managed to get her to come under the bridge; but then for some reason she made a charge for some weeds almost in the canal where perhaps she thought she could hide and gather her composure.

So I stood there, with a lead trailed into a clump of grass and, of course, a lady came up and said where is your dog?

I explained it was my cat and she was there, in the clump of grass.

The lady squeaked in astonishment and said her dog does not like cats.

We watched her small terrier size dog approach and it did not see Silke at all. I even stroked and fussed the happy little dog.

We both chuckled at our little secret, as, off it's lead, it wandered past under the bridge.

A little while later Silke came out and I picked her up as we went back across the bridge. I set her down on the other side on the canal path the way we had come.

She meandered along happily but was obviously a little tired now. She did one of her flops, where she just stops and lays down. So I carried her for a while. Then we rounded a corner and she flopped again. That is when I heard a dog coming fast, like a steam train!

I grabbed Silke just as the dog leapt up to snatch her out of my arms. She lashed out and her claws tore into my arm!

The beagle sized dog kept jumping up. I kept turning so it was wrong sided when it jumped.

Silke all the while was hissing and growling and lashing out. Then I got close to a tree and Silke dived into it.

At that moment an old lady came round the corner chasing after her dog.

She thought I was mad walking a cat but while she was embarrassed that her dog had caused trouble, she did not seem to give a damn about the blood coming down my arm.
I wish people did not encourage their dogs to chase cats.

Silke and I retired to a bench for a brief moment.

She did not want to stay there so I took her back to the hotel where we had a nice relaxing sit down and drew breath in the corner of a beautiful quiet courtyard.
I was able to use some tissues to clean the blood off my arm and Silke relaxed with a small bowl of water while I had a glorious sandwich and got stuck into a gin and

tonic.

The hotel staff were loving their furry visitor, frequently checking on us and making a fuss of Silke. We had the courtyard to ourselves until my friends came back having had a glorious explore and having picked out a place for dinner.

A RUCKSACK?

In the morning the humans have their breakfast and I have mine. Then they take me for a little walk near some castle ruins. I have been here before. I remember it and am happy walking in the familiar woods.

Then we get in the car and drive to a different town. The humans are excited, so I pay attention when we get there. It is an old town called Carcassonne. It is very busy with people.

I am astonished when my human does something he has never done before. He grabs me and stuffs me, none too gently, into a rucksack!
I miaow and protest. I don't like it. I can't get out!
Then he swings the rucksack on to his shoulders with me in it!
With the rucksack on he starts walking!
I miaow and yowl at first. I've never been in a rucksack before and I'm trapped!

But we are amongst so many people. I keep quiet. Too many people.

Eventually we get to a restaurant and the waitress is amazed to see me and says I am the first cat she has had in the restaurant and I am welcome. This is better!

I sit in a corner. My human keeping watch on me. Some human kittens want to touch me. But they cannot get to me as I am in a corner. I don't trust human kittens so I am happy to stay in my corner.

After lunch we split up, my human and I going back to the car. I am in the rucksack again and I'm complaining. What an undignified way for a cat to travel!

When we get to the car, he lets me out. I have a drink of water. Then we go for a walk with my lead and harness this time.

No more rucksack, thank you very much!

—-oooOOOooo—-

POSSIBLY A MISTAKE

Ah the rucksack ...
Knowing that the 'road trip' with my Americans was going to be a bit of a long winded affair, I looked into the idea of a specialist rucksack for Silke so I could walk around with them, with Silke under firm control. In the end I found a friend was selling them.
So I bought one.

It is like a padded computer bag, but has a mesh at the top so that the cat is completely contained within it. The idea is that it can be used for cycling or motorcycling if you so wish.

As I thought we would be walking around places like Carcassonne, an old medieval town with narrow streets and what feels like millions of tourists, I felt it a good plan to fully contain Silke.

I did not have time to train her on this and thought she would be OK about it.

No, she was not.

At Carcassonne I stuffed her into it then shrugged it on and got the others to adjust it. Silke protested loudly. She did not sound excited. She protested.
Among the crowds everyone was staring at this man carrying a protesting cat in a rucksack. At that juncture, one does question whether or not it was the crowds or the narrow streets or the fact that she could not see where she was going.

But what ever it was, she was not happy, and made sure everyone knew it!

We retired to a restaurant and the staff were amazed that I wanted to bring a cat into the place.
"Monsieur this is the first time ever we have a cat here, but yes, I suppose you are welcome."

Fortunately they found us a table in a booth in a corner, so Silke could come out of the rucksack and sit quietly in the corner. Which I'm pleased to say, she did.

As we were paying our bill, two small french children wanted to pet her. She got agitated about this and I could see trouble as they were trying to get under the table to get at her.

I could see a look in Silke's eye that said 'you touch me I scratch you, I don't trust you!'
Time to leave. It was agreed I would go back to the car with Silke and they could all properly go and explore Carcassonne. This being the old medieval part of Car-

cassonne which feels like knights should be arriving on horses in shining armour at any moment, to meet swooning damsels, I expected them to be some time.

Due to Silke's protest and her absolute horror of going in the rucksack again, I resorted to the lead and harness, but with so many people around she could not walk out as either she would have been trodden on or would have tripped someone up.

So a compromise was reached and she rode out of Carcassonne like a recently rescued damsel on the shoulder of her knight, with people cooing at how cute she was and she, acknowledging her public, but being quiet and happy enough at the experience.

Once outside the town and away from the coaches, which she regards as no better than big trucks, she was happy enough to come to the car and take a drink.
Food? not interested.
So I walked her to the end of the car park where there was a nice grassy bank, and suddenly, to my horror, she fought off and slipped out of her harness!

This was the first time she had ever done that, and promptly bolting under a fence and into some bushes where she lay up, she refused to come out and stubbornly stayed put, no doubt de-stressing.

Even though I was cross and wanted to shout at her, that would have been pointless and likely to scare her further. So I lay on the grass and waited, occasionally calling her softly.

Of course I had been very worried as to how to get her out of those bushes from behind a stout chain-link fence, but eventually she came out and, with many head bumps and rubbings, she kinda said sorry.

So the harness went back on and was adjusted a little tighter this time.

We sat on the grass together until I saw my friends coming back, when we sauntered back to the car to meet them.

To Silke it was as though nothing had happened.
All was good with the world as far as she was concerned.

Nothing to see here!

---oooOOOooo---

CHAPTER 8

Silke's Second Christmas in England

The weather was getting a little cooler, and the winds were stronger. I knew winter was coming to Spain.

Pedro the builder still came quite regularly doing jobs around the house, but nothing big. He always makes me fight with him, I am gentle but use my war cries as I kill his hand. I am very fierce in this game. But I hold back my claws and don't bite hard as I know it is a game.

The villa now has central heating, and it is warm and cosy. The rain and wind are outside, there are no draughts. I have my cat door and come and go as I please. I am the only cat that comes in through this door. Other cats may try, but it will not work for them. For me, when I approach, it gives a squeak and lets me in. It is my personal door.

The human had got a suitcase out. I then noticed boxes in the hallway.

He kept talking about going to England again.

Then he took me to see Rosa the vet. She checked me over, but did not prick me this time, and then stamped the little blue book which is all about me and the humans call my passport.

The next day the car was loaded.
My human left the doors open so I could inspect the car, all my things were in there, so I knew we were off on our travels.
I was excited and frisked around in the garden.

I did not want to leave just yet. Who would keep an eye on Pedro and the men? But my human caught me, put me in the car, closed the doors, and we were off!

I yowled.
I yowled at the window, I yowled at the mountain disappearing behind us, I yowled at the dogs barking in their yards, I yowled at the human.
But I wasn't scared, I was excited. We were going on another adventure.

When we turned out of the small roads onto the main road, I came and nuzzled my human then settled into my basket. This is my high level travel basket, made just for me. I can see out, I am happy.

Soon we joined the big fast roads through the toll barrier. When the car was nearly at the barrier there was a squeak, then the barrier went up and the traffic light turned green. I miaow. Stop squeaking and let us through!

The big trucks were growling along. What a horrible noise they make.
I stared at them to make sure we passed them safely.
There is no problem, they never chase us and we are much faster anyway, but I just don't like them. We passed them quickly.

I knew this journey would be long so I stretched and washed and settled down to snooze.

After a few hours we stopped and gave the car its smelly drink.

We parked the car and my human got out.
He got a coffee and a sandwich. Humans can't go for long without coffee, it seems to me.

We moved the car to a quieter place and opened the door so that I could get out, but I could not go not far as I was tied onto the car with my harness on.

Then we went for a little walk on some grass. Suddenly I saw big trucks and I was scared. I wanted to run back to the car. My human knows I do not like big trucks.

It was getting dark now and we had been driving all day. The mountains in the distance had snow on the top. We had been through many tolls, and passed many big trucks. The border crossing from Spain into France was clear and free so we drove through without stopping, then we changed roads, leaving the big road behind.

Box Woman kept talking to us at roundabouts and junctions. My human told her off as she always gets this bit wrong, and he knows that.
'Shut up, box woman!' I yelled.
Then she said …..."recalculating"….. and we are happy again because she went quiet.

This road is just two way and winds across the French countryside into the night.
I settled down on my cushion and only sat up and took any notice when we went through villages.
The villages were pretty with Christmas lights across the narrow streets, I like those lights.

Finally we came to a little village and turned off the main road into the narrow road that runs up into the mountains. I knew where I was!
Then we came to the house where the lovely man and woman live, the ones with the big dog called Athos.

Athos rushed out to meet us, all barking and slobber. I hissed at him. He's not a bad dog and is OK with we cats, but I still don't want him to get too close.

My stuff was put in the same room we have stayed in before and my human went down for dinner.

I was so happy. Cats like routine, you see. I knew this place. I was comfortable and fell into a nice sleep knowing my human would come up soon.
A little later, when he went to sleep, I snuggled up on the bed next to him.

In the morning we set off again. We said our good-byes to the lovely man and woman and Athos the dog.
Athos was limping a little, he is old and has arthritis.

That day passed in a blur of stops for fuel, tolls, and trucks being passed.

—-oooOOOooo—-

We stopped at a small hotel in the middle of no-where. I was on my harness and made it as difficult as possible for my human to go where he wanted to go, as I wanted to explore.
We argued and I pulled hard on the harness until he picked me up and carried me.

This hotel was old but the room was nice and warm.

In the morning I wanted a walk, but there was nowhere convenient for us to go. Instead we drove away from the old hotel into the frozen French countryside. I wondered why it was so quiet, perhaps it was a Saturday morning when humans are sluggish and don't get up early if they don't have to.

There was a light mist, and it was cold and frosty but the lazy humans were missing a lovely morning.

We got to the Channel Tunnel and my human put me into my basket. Once again we went in to see the vet which is not a vet (well, not like Rosa). There was no one in front of us and my special passport book was checked and we were good to go. Unfortunately, on the way out a boisterous dog wanted to stick its nose in my cage, so I hissed and tried to scratch his nose.

I was happy to get back on my travel box and cushion as we went through the check points, where some of the humans looked at me sitting in the car or standing at the dashboard and smiled. People like to see a travelling cat, it seems.

We didn't have to wait long this time and soon drove onto the train.

The engine was turned off and we relaxed in the car. I sat on my human's lap.

There was lots of noise from people speaking excitedly as the train began to move, so I hid in my travel box which was like a cave under all the stuff on the back seat.

No one can see me here. I refused to come out.

At the other end though, when we drove off the train, I returned to my travel box. I like to see what is going on.

My human started off by driving gently, letting the cars who were more aggressive and anxious go first and get away from us, then he eased the car into the traffic flow and we cruised along as usual.

It was raining, the wipers were on and we were driving on a different side of the road.

The roads were wide but very busy and progress was slow, but I was warm and dry and safe with my human. Slip slop ... slip slop ... The car knows what to do, quietly humming away. It made me feel drowsy again.

But I was soon awake and alert again when we reached the quieter roads. The adventure was about to begin!

RAIN, BUT NOT IN SPAIN

*O*ur journey to the Channel Tunnel from our last stop was fairly uneventful and there were only short queues to drive onto the train for a change, but the weather in England was bad.

Our destination, near Dorking in Surrey, involved tackling the M25 motorway, which even on a Saturday was busy.

The rain was sloshing down and the wipers were constantly on, slipping and slopping. The spray coming up from the vehicles made the driving more challenging. Silke was happier though when we reached the Reigate area and the rain eased.

It had all but stopped when we reached the Leatherhead and Dorking exit where we left the motorway behind; and on the tree lined A24, where we were a lot slower, she paid attention and watched the wet countryside pass by.

There is a huge metal sculpture of a chicken in the middle of the roundabout near Dorking.

The story goes that the 'Dork' is a large breed of chicken and it seems the local council decided it was a suitable emblem to mark the entrance to the town.

For us, though, it signified that the end of our journey was close.

A NEW ADVENTURE

I consulted my diary for further notes about this trip ... What? I told you cats kept diaries ... didn't you believe me?
This is what I found ...

We are in English countryside and although winter is here it is beautiful.
We stop in a town, in a supermarket car park. I am left in the car and I am not happy about it.

My human comes out with a rattly wheeled cart loaded with shopping, he loads it into the car and, spotting my chance, I try to get out of the car. But he will not let me. Sometimes I want to bite him.

Then he starts the car and we try to get out of the car park.

A lady with her nose in the air pushes a laden cart straight out in front of us making us stop. As she opens the back of her big black car (a 'four wheel drive Chelsea tractor', according to my human) to load it, she is blocking the road completely. She is making us wait!

My human sits patiently, stuck, and there are more cars behind us.

Suddenly she realises how rude she is being to so many people, looks up and sees me driving the car.

She is shocked. She dithers and stares at me again before she realises my human is driving and the steering wheel is on the other side!

She sheepishly moves her cart out of the way and with a polite wave my human cruises past. I stare at her, turning my head as we go by as I stand up at the dashboard, she stares back.

'Silly thoughtless woman' I miaow at her. The drivers of other cars behind us mouth curses and wave fists at her for being so rude.

We drive out of the town on country roads in the rain. slip ... slop, slip ... slop ... Squeak! The rain is stopping so my human turns off the noisy wipers.

We drive into a nice place. There are wooden cabins around and that soft green English grass.

I wait in the car a short while as my human goes to see a man in a hut and then we drive to a cabin.

There, finally I am allowed out. My lead is unhooked and while my human unloads the car stuff into the cabin, I run and jump, and explore this new place.

The rain had stopped but now it starts afresh and I rush inside to find that my human had prepared food for me, which I enjoy. Then we sit down and he watches the TV while I watch the rain.

It is a small but very nice place, and my human has arranged my things just as I like them.

We are cosy, warm and dry.

I am happy.

I love my human, I sleep on his bed.

---oooOOOooo---

Next morning it is cold and frosty and I don't want to go in the car so I yowl.

We don't go far. He takes me to an area of woods and common land and we go for a walk with me running free without the harness, I love the smells and sounds.

I listen to the birds and rustle the dead leaves.

We follow small footpaths.

I like it. I am happy.

My human walks slowly so I don't get lost. Sometimes I run ahead. But never far. He knows this
place and I do not.

He stops often so that I can pause and take in all
that I see and smell. I like that.

We wander.

Suddenly he rushes to me and picks me up holding
me tight!

'Dog', he says quietly.

There are in fact two, and at least the dog walkers
have put them on leads so that they do not

frighten me. The dog walkers are impressed that I am going for a walk and stop to talk.

People don't seem to take cats for walks in England. Mind you, now I come to think about it, I don't think they do in France or Spain either. Odd things, humans.

These dogs are small and just sniff around my human's feet, then off they go, tails wagging and once far enough away, their walkers let them off their leads.

My human puts me down and we find a wide path that is chewed up with light sandy dirt.

After a short while we turn onto a grassy area to one side. I like this place with its green grass and rustling leaves.
When I look up, my human has crossed the grassy area and is nearly at the car. I hear it first....

A thunderous pounding of the ground ... lots of heavy huffing and puffing ... and its getting closer very quickly!

I am terrified. What ever is it?!
I bound towards my human in my biggest leaps. I see him and the car but I cannot get to the car in time before the sound seems to be almost on top of me. So quickly reviewing my options, I rush under a bush to hide.

Almost as suddenly as it started the noise stops,

and walking quietly into the car park is a horse and rider. No longer galloping, thank goodness.

My human opens the car door, but I am watching that horse and not about to go anywhere.
Never have I seen such a big creature and when it was galloping, it moved so fast!

When I think it is safe I run with my belly on the ground into the safety of the car, I watch the horse walk off into the woods. My human tries to calm me down but I am too scared for that. I am all fluffed up.

I am really pleased to be inside the wooden cabin again when we get back. This scary escapade has left me exhausted so my human leaves me to sleep.

—-oooOOOooo—-

There is no cat flap for me to use (but I have my dirt box) so when my human is around he opens the front door for me, but when he is out I am inside sleeping and cozy.

I can watch dogs on leads go by, I can watch birds flying around, there are many more birds in England than in Spain. A window is better than TV for me.
Every day we go for a walk to the same place, I love it. I love my human and am glad we go on such ad-

ventures together.

It is that special time for humans and as Christmas day comes we watch TV.

There is a film on called "How to train your dragon". I didn't know about dragons. I do know about cats and I think the main character is a badly drawn cat.
I watch it happily, but I don't believe the story-line.

TV is strange. Creatures on there seem to come into the house but they have no smell, and sometimes there is music so I cannot hear what sound the creatures make.
But I like 'How to train your dragon'. I think it is really a story about a cat that can fly.

In the morning my human packs the car, I jump in happily knowing we are going home, and we set off on our journey back to Spain.

My human looks at me and I look at him. I try to tell him we have each other and will never be parted, and he tells me he loves me.

—-oooOOOooo—

We stay at a beautiful hotel in France called Les Etangs de Guibert.
Etang in French means a wild fresh water lake. And there is a lake!

It has ducks and geese on it but we arrived in the dark and left early so I cannot tell you much about the lake this time.

We stop the car in a forest full of tall beech trees. It is frosty and cold. The leaves on the ground are beech leaves. They are cold on my paws and go crunch when I walk on them.

I try to not walk on them as they are very cold but I have several paws and at least some need to be on the ground.

My human chuckles as he thinks it looks as though I am dancing.

It is cold, so we don't stay long and go back to the car. My human turns on the heater and, cosy and warm again, we set off to the Pyrenees mountains.

We drive all day and then stay with the lovely humans and Athos the dog again.

There are other guests at La Folie tonight. They have come on horses!

I watch them with their horses from the window. I still can't make my mind up about horses.

At dusk, a something visits the garden outside. I growl my most serious growl. It is a big something, the size of a large cat ... and it jumps through the long grass. I do not know what it is but I don't like it. My human is excited and says it is a pine marten and very rare. The rarer the better as far as I'm concerned!

But this is a big evening for wildlife and next the wild boar come to eat. Big ones and small boar kittens. I growl with menace at them too.

---oooOOOooo---

—-oooOOOooo—-

The next day we arrive home in Spain, late in the evening. I am happy to be home. It is warm and there is no rain.

I dream of my adventures, of passing trucks and toll barriers. I dream of my short walk in the woods near where Athos lives. I dream of the birds in England, and the song they make, and the smells of the dead leaves in the woods. I dream of the soft English grass. I dream of the journey. I dream of frozen leaves and the wonderful sights and sounds of the forest. I dream of being a flying cat.

I love my forever human, and thanks to him, I am a well travelled cat.

---oooOOOooo---

THE MOUNTAIN HOUSE

I needed to move out of the villa for the summer to take advantage of lucrative summer rentals.

Where to go? It made sense if I moved away from the coast, so Jalon and surrounding areas came to mind.

I started asking around.

Through a friend I found a mountain house at the top of Bernia I could rent.

Living in one of these is almost an off grid experience. Electricity is from solar panels only. The fridge runs off gas and so does the shower.
There was enough electricity only for the phone charger and the computer. Nothing else was possible.

Lighting was by battery flashlight. Thankfully it was summer so no need for heating, or it would have been log fires only.

Drinkable water comes up on a truck to these remote places ... and waste water also goes down on a truck.

You have to hope you don't meet one of those coming the other way on the narrow mountain roads!

The house was cute and perfect, being well enough back so that Silke was unlikely to run out into the road.

In the morning there would be visits from quail, Strange birds who make lots of clucking noises and Silke eyes them with interest, wondering, no doubt, how they would fit beneath her skin.

At night wild boar would be on the prowl.

And a 'podenco'. These are large dogs in the style of greyhounds, used in the"Campo", as the Spanish countryside is called, for hunting rabbits and other eatables.

Sadly the hunters abuse them terribly even though they are often sweet natured dogs.

The one that started roaming around our mountain hideaway had a broken front leg, but could still move at a heck of a pace.

Silke had to have some way of entering and exiting the house so I installed a hook to secure the window, allowing just enough room for her to come and go. It was safe enough from human intruders as the window was also fitted with bars.

Once I came home late at night, enjoying a joyous top down drive under the stars in the soft embrace of the warm summer night, up the mountain road. When I arrived there was no sign of Silke. After a while of calling I heard a faint Miaow. I started searching and calling her and found her high up a tree.

A ladder was needed to recover her.

I was disturbed again later when the podenco came calling again; and there was a kerfuffle of yowls and screams from Silke by the window as the dog tried to climb in to catch and eat her.

My friend Cachita came to the rescue and stirred up some animal charities who tracked down the man who owned the dog. He came looking for it and eventually caught it, and it disappeared to goodness knows what fate.

The police had had a word with him and he said that he lost the dog just four days beforehand. That can't have been true as it was running around for weeks up there.

The story eventually emerged that the hunter had thrown the dog out on the mountain with a broken leg to fend for itself. Many podencos suffer similar and sometimes much worse fates.
In the autumn the boar hunters shoot and poison any podencos they encounter running wild, so that they can hunt the boar. If they did not, then the wounded abandoned podencos would hunt the piglets.

Many Spanish people abhor how badly the campo

(country) Spanish treat animals and, of course the ex-pats hate it and worry about their pets being shot or poisoned. It is a perennial problem in rural Spain.

Apart from that Silke throughly enjoyed living there!

There were some bushes and scrub that the quail might be found in, and a vineyard which rabbits often visited. She would chase the rabbits but by the time she pounced they were long gone.
Wild rabbits do not stop to play games with cats. Life for them leaves no time for games.

Thunderstorms, up in the mountains are spectacular. You feel very close to them. Remarkably, however, Silke is not at all unnerved by thunderstorms.

Most nights she would curl up contentedly in her bed in a corner of my bedroom.

We had a basement too, if the door was open Silke would be down there in a flash to explore.

Next door there was a restaurant, sadly plagued with wasps and we had to suffer the wasps too. Very annoying when breakfast, if taken on the patio, included a sea view in the distance.
Cachita provided those electric bug swatters and we had fun if eating outside batting the irritating but very persistent things away.

Silke developed a comical technique in the car, on the twisty mountain roads. She would brace herself with one paw on the dashboard and one on the door.

Every evening we would walk around the vineyard and the scrub, she loved it.

Sometimes I came home to be greeted by her leaping out of a low olive tree where she had been dozing. Other times she would gallop up out of the vineyard.

Even though the entrance to the house was firmly marked 'Private' cars would often come up the drive to park for the restaurant next door. People would then try to cross the soft earth of the vineyard and finally encounter a bramble patch before having to go back to their cars to find the proper restaurant entrance.

Cyclists too would regularly appear out of nowhere looking to steal water. Outside taps have to be turned off inside the house to prevent this cheeky but all too common practice.

When the drinking water has to be hauled up the mountain roads on expensive trucks, the commodity is precious and needs careful guarding!

There was a very specific system which had to be followed when living in this remote place. If you went down the mountain you carefully planned all you had to do, because once you were back up you were unlikely to want to come down again.

It took nearly twenty five minutes to get up there from Jalon on the very twisty road.

The road was also made dangerous by other users. The worst perhaps being gangs of cyclists coming down at ridiculous speeds, clearly unable to stop, and treating the road like their private 'Tour de France' race track.

NOW I LIVE ON A MOUNTAIN!

Strange birds make strange clucking noises outside. They are birds that do not fly much and are quite big. The human says they are guinea fowl. I wonder if they are tasty.

This place is different and there is no pool for me to drink from.
There is a vineyard next door and we walk in it in the evening.
There is often a rustle in the grass and just as I am about to pounce on it, a rabbit races off.

I land where the rabbit was. I look to see its white tail disappear in the bushes. My human is chuckling. I twitch my tail in anger. I missed.
I remember the one in England in the garden, but this one does not want to play. I remember all our travels.

We are still travelling in a way. We have not gone

back to the villa in ages, and whilst we are still in Spain we are far away, high up in the mountains and staying in a little house next door to a restaurant.

I like it here, apart from the wasps. But there is a dog that won't leave me alone.

I was outside beyond the yard when this big dog surprised me. I could not get back to the house so I raced up a pine tree into the branches.

It tried to jump and get me, but it had hurt its leg and it could not reach. Dogs can't climb trees. I will not be its supper tonight.

But being up the tree caused another problem.

When my human came home, long after the dog had gone, he could not find me. He called and called then came looking with a light.

I could hear him, of course, so I miaowed and chirruped until he finally looked up and spotted me up the tree.

I know it's silly but I could not get down. It was too high to jump, and I know I should, but I didn't want to have to come down the tree backwards even though I know that's the way our claws work.

Coming down head first the claws won't grip, but coming down backwards is so undignified and you can't see who is below ... and who might bite your bottom!

I was stuck and I was so glad my human was there to rescue me.

He got a ladder, reached up and clutched me. I didn't struggle. I knew I was safe.

Once he got me down, I ran happily into the house to eat my supper and lick sticky pine resin off my fur.

—oooOOOooo—-

CHAPTER 9

Silke moves house again.

It was a spring evening and the weather was beginning to warm up when my human got out the quiet blue car with the steering wheel on the wrong side. I burst out of the door nearly tripping him up to see what he was doing.

He invited me to come in the car, I was not sure. He waited. Then he opened the passenger door so I jumped in and I went straight to the back parcel shelf so he could not get me out easily.

As we drove off I came forwards and stood at the dashboard. Anyone coming the other way would think a cat was driving the car.

We turned off in an unusual place and went through a small Spanish town. I yowled as I like to do in towns. I like looking at the doors and windows, the people drinking at cafes, the shops, and the traffic.

We left the town on a wide but twisty road as we climbed through a steep gorge.

Then we turned off into another town and on to another wide twisty road, still climbing.

After some more turns we started to go down a wide but steep road towards the sea. We eventually came down to an area called La Fustera where there are pine forests.

I am cat. I do not know these names, but my human does. My descriptions of these places would not be understood by humans. I could tell you about smells and birds and trees, but not road signs and place names.

This journey took maybe thirty minutes in a car, but it might take me, just on my paws, several days. Cars are amazing, and they eat up great distances in no time, which is why I like travelling with my human in them.

From the coast road we turned into the pine forests with villas nestling between the trees.

Then we took another turn and went down a steep small road, finally turning into a gateway at a villa.

My human stopped the car, shut off the engine and opened the door. Before he could get out I was out checking the place over.

Immediately there was a miaow and I answered with my 'transient cat' yowl. We do this if we are off territory and have no wish for a territory fight. It is the same long yowl I use when we drive through towns.

The other cat was immediately curious but not screaming war.

My human called me to follow him upstairs and another human man appeared and greeted him. We got to the front door at the same time to be greeted by a lady with a strong voice. The two humans greeted me too, but then a dog appeared.

It was a very old dog and seemed to be almost blind. It was not making a noise, just sniffing, I was curious, I had never met an old dog before.
We almost touched noses. But then I smelled the cat food! I went straight for it and stared to eat.

The humans poured wine and laughed and talked as happy humans do.

An aggressive growly yowl came from behind me. I whipped round to be confronted by the resident cat, 'Stripey'.
She was old and skinny, and typical of many Spanish cats, she had blue eyes, a chocolate head, a creamy body but a tabby cat tail. That tail is why she is called Stripey.
She was not happy that I had the temerity to be

there, either. It seems I was eating her food!

I backed away cautiously and went off to explore with her following.
Then the humans called me and we went downstairs to what in Spain is often called an underbuild.

In other places it might be the basement flat. It was on ground level, the same as the car, the garage, and the pool with the villa built over the top of it.
My human had to duck to get in, but once in could just stand up in what was a small studio flat.

We went back upstairs and the humans sat down to dinner. I sat quietly on a chair next to my human. I was the perfect guest not bothering for food.

Stripey was not amused I was still there and after dinner when the humans were chatting, she ambushed me.
This was our first fight of many. She had long legs so could swipe me and rake me with her claws, but if I got in close she got bitten and scratched. It was, however, a very brief encounter and got Stripey's humans yelling at her.

The humans declared it was time to go and I followed my human out and got in the quiet blue car. We made our way home, I noticed how different it all was at night with lights twinkling everywhere.

—-oooOOOooo—-

A few weeks later and suddenly my things were in the normal car, our adventure car, and we were off to the same little flat.

When my human got out my food bowl I knew we were staying. To make it easier for me to get in and out, he removed a small pane of glass from a window in the tiny galley kitchen so that I could come and go as I pleased.

I wondered how long we would be staying here.

—-oooOOOooo—-

The summer days passed with my human coming and going.

Stripey and I made our feelings known towards each other with yowl offs. If she came in through the open window to steal my food she would get attacked and chased out, especially as she peed on everything every time she came in to tell me this was her territory.

Other cats came to feed here and the humans put food out for them. Sometimes they left the kitchen door open, and I could go and steal Stripey's food. But *I* did not pee on everything.

The old dog was called Milly and I met her occasionally. She did not bother me, nor I her. But I could smell that she was not well.

Unfortunately one day she died. Everyone was very sad and crying, including my human. The other man human had dug a hole in the garden and he buried her there. The lady human was distraught, she loved Milly very much and I was sorry for her.

—-oooOOOooo—-

There was a pool which I liked to lie beside until it got too hot.
Of course the pool was great to drink from too.

I had always worried about my human going into pools, but here I quite liked it when he went swimming, because he would play with me at the edge.

I was not stupid enough to go in the pool myself, of course.

It was just fascinating to play swipe at my human's hand or fingers. My human is very quick but sometimes I win and grab him.
I don't hurt him though, its just a game.

The two humans upstairs, shouted at me.

I did not like that.

This occurred when I went to steal Stripey's food or settle down in their company; and if for some reason
they didn't want me there, they would shout at me.

I would get scared when they shouted and nip or swat their ankles with a little bit of claws out.

They started to call me 'spawn of satan' (devil's child)! Who me?

—-oooOOOooo—-

On one occasion a dog and its owners came to visit. It was a nice friendly dog called Max. He was not especially big and had quite short legs.
Max came strolling into the apartment following his nose towards my food, which meant he had to come right into the galley kitchen.

At the time I was asleep outside but when he went in the door I galloped in behind him. I attacked from behind and he turned tail and ran back up the stairs to the salon and terrace above where the guests were, I pressed home the attack swatting his backside, and he yelped like a real wimp.

The humans got Max in and shut me out. So I stood outside the window making my best blood curdling yowls.

Moments later my human came to get me. He did not scold me, but I don't think he was very pleased.

—-oooOOOooo—-

It was about this time, that my human discovered the people upstairs were afraid to pick me up.

He would have to come and get me as I do not like being picked up and tend to go into death hug mode as an automatic reaction.

That means I bite, while hugging with my front paws and using my front claws, while rabbit kicking with claws out from my back feet.

Many is the time my human was asked to come and remove the 'spawn of satan' by the people upstairs.

The summer got hotter, and I found some fabulous new places to lie up. Like the shower for the pool which was just so cool and shady.

There were some trees as well, with a soft bed of needles to lie on. But ants and mosquitoes would frequently bite.

I learnt shady stones were the best place to be cool, but the patio table chairs pushed under the table were good too, comfy and shady.

I had a fight with Stripey.
She bit me and I got an abscess. I felt unwell.

My human took me to see Rosa the vet. She pricked me and afterwards I slept longer than usual.
But I felt good afterwards and the abscess went.

This often happens when cats bite each other.

NOW, I MUST TELL YOU ABOUT MY TAIL.

My tail is mine. It expresses many of my emotions and how I feel about things. I use it for balance when I'm climbing and hunting.

I hate it being played with. When kittens play with their mother's tail, they get bashed.

If I am hunting and trying to be very still and

quiet, the tip of my tail will often twitch.

If I am coming to say hello to you, it will be straight up in the air.

If I am really pleased to see you, it might be up in the air but gently swishing side to side as well. That is about as close to a dog wagging its tail as I want to get.

If its twitching more than just the tip, then I am agitated and might be cross about something. In which case look out! I might be about to bite or scratch!

Stripey was dozing on a chair under the patio table, her tail hanging down. I swiped at her tail, she woke up and yowled, I yowled back. We had a brief fight and she went off upstairs.
I was glad about that. I like being the patio cat, Stripey can go back upstairs to the humans that shout at me.

—-oooOOOooo—-

All summer long I lazed around, slept peacefully, had the occasional cat chase and stand off, dug up the humans vegetables to do my business, and found shady spots to lie up and watch the world.

At night I slept on my human's bed.

He took me for walks but there were not many interesting places to go for either of us even though the pine trees were nice and cool and shady and I liked the smell of them.

He took me down the sea once. I did not like it and got back in the car. I felt so exposed. There is nowhere to hide.

—-oooOOOooo—-

Builders, with big machines and trucks, arrived on the empty land next door. They quickly erected a house. What my human disparagingly calls an Ibiza box. In his opinion it was just a human box. No wonder it went up so fast.

My human makes lovely food on the thing called the barbecue. I don't like chicken much. But if he cuts me off a little raw chicken I will relish it.
I like pork chops too. Steak I am so-so about. But I love the barbecue.

The humans upstairs come down to join us. There is much human laughter. I like it when humans laugh and talk.

When I was young, food was hard to find. I was often hungry. Now my human always makes sure I have enough to eat. I always have biscuits in my bowl, fresh water and twice a day I get tinned stuff as well. I particularly like Sheba cat food. I really don't like much else. But my human is very tolerant. He knows I am fussy.

—-oooOOOooo—-

I quickly made my mark with the family of cats living here. I was not to be messed with. Only Stripey did not get that message.

Once there was a three way cat fight. I was involved and we went hurtling across the road, screaming and yelling at each other before sorting out our differences in a nearby garden. It helped establish me as top cat.

—-oooOOOooo—-

My human often watches videos. He put on some with animals for me. I love them. I want to be in that place where the animals are.

When I look behind the screen there is only the box he calls the computer.

I cannot smell the place where the animals are or birds, mice, squirrels and the rabbits on the shiny screen.

I like watching the computer. But not for too long.

When my human went to bed and I prepared to sleep, it was the dead of night; but I watched Stripey sneak in through the open window, sliding behind the net curtain!
She made straight for my food bowl!

I gave a warning grumble and growl then, as she turned to face me I made a long rising yowl.
I wanted to make it clear I was not having this so my next yowl became a shriek, at which point I pounced!

Stripey was knocked over. I may be small but I am well fed and quite substantial enough to do some damage if I choose to.

We fought hard. Biting, scratching, rabbit kicking with our back feet, and rolled around on the floor.

Cowardly Stripey bolted out of the kitchen window with me in hot pursuit. We tore off up the garden and had a yowl off at each other up the hilly garden with Stripey under a bush.

Eventually I let her make a slow walking retreat.
I watched her go upstairs and onto the terrace, along a precarious ledge to a different more inaccessible patio she liked to sleep on, and where

she had a box she curled up in.

She thought she was safe there from me.
I was not finished with her yet!

But that ledge was so narrow only a thin thing like Stripey could fit. I was too fat!

Previously, if the doors were open inside and I was in the house, I would go and see if she was there. Even if she was not, she would smell I had visited.

I swished my tail.

Of course I had woken my human but the fight had happened so fast there was very little he could do particularly as we were outside.

So after a while he went back to sleep.

I crept in a little later and of course I was there when he woke up so he could feed me.

---oooOOOooo---

The humans upstairs fed me tuna fish occasionally.

My human does not give me tuna fish like that, the stuff he gets is oily and I don't like it. This is salty and clear and delicious.
But humans can learn and soon my human gave me the same. I was delighted. He has learned his lesson well.

The humans upstairs yelled at me when I stole Stripey's food. What is all the fuss about? She steals mine if she gets the chance, so why not? But upstairs they yell at me and chase me out.

I nip their ankles. "Spawn of Satan", they yell at me.
I don't like their harsh voices so I run downstairs

to the apartment. I don't know what they mean or why they are cross with me.

My human often gives me ham. I have discovered there are many different types of ham. Some I like more than others.

I do not like chicken, unless, as I said, my human chops off some small pieces he is about to barbecue, or sometimes when he has cooked it (I may have already mentioned that!).
I like barbecued pork chops too.

—-oooOOOooo—-

The man upstairs kept a big shiny black car in the garage. He often spent hours cleaning and polishing it.
One day it was in my way so, naturally enough, I walked over it. He yelled 'spawn of satan!' at me and chased me off!

I was sitting with the lady upstairs on another occasion and she tried to move me, I did not like that so rabbit kicked her and nipped her. After that she was frightened to sit next to me.

My human started packing boxes soon after these incidents. Then he packed my things and we said goodbye.

—-oooOOOooo—-

I was not sure how far we were going and it was evening. We don't usually start on an adventure in the evening.

We were in a town in traffic when suddenly we got bumped from behind by another car! My human told me to stay in the car. He and the man who had bumped us shouted at each other. I hid. I had had enough of shouting.

Then my human got back in the car and drove away.

We drove up a steep road and arrived in a quiet residential area with pine trees and palms everywhere. There were large villas set into the mountainside and I could see gardens and woods.

My human reversed up a small narrow road amongst some nice smart buildings. It seemed we had arrived and when he opened the door I jumped out to see where I was.

He unpacked the car and went through a small open hallway and into an apartment. Something told me this was going to be home. My food was here and I had a cat door in the window a little way off the ground. I was happy.

I started to explore this new domain but then heard my human start the car and drive it away! But it was all right, I need not have worried. It has a very distinctive rattly engine note and I heard it nearby, seeming to come from underground, beneath the apartment.

I found some stairs going down, and at the bottom I miaowed loudly, my human opened a door, and there was the car in its own house with many other cars!

This place needed careful exploring but my human caught me and told me 'not tonight'.

We went back up into the apartment and I discovered it had a balcony.

It was a curious arrangement, as the entrance door and my cat flap were on the ground floor at the front, but the balcony was on the first floor at the back.

I realised it had been built into the mountainside and the balcony looked out over fields towards the sea.

It all seemed very pleasant to me. It was much bigger than the studio under Stripeys house and had areas of garden on all sides.

It was certainly very comfortable and I started to settle in.

—-oooOOOooo—-

CHAPTER 10
Change: the only certainty

My plan was to rent the villa out, either for holidays or on a more permanent basis, so Silke and I had to move.

Fortunately we did not have to go far and I secured a very pleasant apartment on a rather up-market urbanisation nearby.
The setting was charming, with well kept gardens and a delightful view towards the sea and the mountains beyond the avocado and orange trees, where we were treated to spectacular sunsets.

It was pretty safe for Silke too, and although the gardens were not for our exclusive use, a cursory inspection revealed only one dog in residence in the small low rise block. But with the apartments arranged so that only four were served off each entrance, and as the dog's place was approached by a different stair, Silke should be safe enough.

The dog in question wasn't much bigger than Silke, so, as I arranged to fit a cat flap in a window a little above the ground overlooking a secluded grassed area. I was convinced she would soon settle.

ON THE MOVE

When you are a well travelled cat living in Spain and, in my present life at least, (did I mention that cats have nine lives at their disposal?), somewhat pampered; moving from place to place holds no fear for me.

It is August in Spain and this year it is very hot and humid.

I now live with my forever human in a modest apartment, it is on the ground floor at the front and first floor at the back. This means I can do what I like to do best, sleep safely and soundly, occasionally waking up to see what is going on. I can also go out through my special cat door into the garden whenever I want.

It is not as quiet or as large as our villa, but it is quite a bit larger than the studio and, with no Stripey to disturb the peace, makes a perfectly acceptable domicile.

I have also quickly established my position in the local cat hierarchy as top cat.

I have had to quell some local discontent, particularly from the ruffians who live down by the
bridge, but generally my human and I have settled
in well.

—-oooOOOooo—-

I had just come in after something of a difference
of opinion with one of the uncouth strays down
by the bridge and, seeking comfort and succour
and space to lick the fairly inconsequential nick
or two I had sustained during the debate, I decided
to curl up on the squashy thing by my human's
feet.
I thought he was asleep, but I was mistaken, and he
had the effrontery to try to move me away!
I was just closing my eyes, so his action surprised
me and I had to growl ... one of my deep warning
ones, to get him to desist.

But, would you believe it, he did not stop and carried me off and dumped me unceremoniously on the sofa.

I was not happy.

I strutted to my bed instead, to show my displeasure.
I know perfectly well where my own bed is, thank you very much, but on this occasion I wanted to sleep on the best bit of the squashy thing, which is down by his feet!

I got my own way in the end, of course. During the night, using my silent paws, I padded back into the bedroom and took up my station as before on the squashy thing. And that is where he found me when he awoke in the morning.

That will teach him!

—-oooOOOooo—-

We still go for walks in the same places although sometimes we go somewhere new. There are plenty of places to walk around this new home.

He takes me to strange woods but always knows where we are going and I don't worry about getting lost.
He stops and waits for me if I get too far behind.

I like to dawdle sometimes, and smell the scents

of wild boar and rabbits as well as the flowers and the earth. Then I have to catch up.
He keeps a look out for dogs too and comes to get me and puts me on his shoulder if a dog is around.
My human always keeps me safe.

For the last few weeks the urbanisation has been busy with people, some with young children. The swimming pool where I like to drink in particular has been full of noisy boisterous children.
People have been inconsiderately walking past the apartment all day long in squeaky flip-flops.

A French man and woman stayed in the apartment upstairs. She was always shouting angrily at the man. I would look at my human for comfort and a reassuring stroke. I did not like all this anger.

A small dog came on holiday with a Spanish family. They would leave it at home for hours, it would cry and howl and bark. It was so lonely and unhappy.

But my favourite family visits regularly next door, they are Spanish. When I hear them, I race out through the cat door to say hello. They are kind and gentle.
The young teenage girls study hard and like to sit on the steps in the hallway to do homework.
I like to sit with them.
They are such a beautiful family. I have explored their apartment. It is very clean and tidy.

I did look under the beds to be sure!

Suddenly, there is nobody here. The little complex of apartments has maybe three permanent residents. The pool is quiet and I can drink there again. The loudest noises are the birds.

There are no chattering voices, radios or children playing. Just the sounds of nature.

I like to sit on the bathroom window sill.
I watch birds hunting in the long grass in the field next door. The swallows are my favourite, with their speed and aerobatics.

I like to sleep on the balcony too. From there I can watch the blood red Spanish sunsets over the mountains, and the beautiful grey dawns.
I listen to the music of the birdsong in the avocado and orange fields next door.

I watch the twinkling lights down by the sea in the distance at night.

Sometimes a zephyr of breeze rattles the leaves of the big palm tree by the balcony.

I like it here.

We travelling cats have a saying;
'Wherever my human is, that's my home'.

—-oooOOOooo—-

NEW HABITS

Since we moved to this Spanish apartment, my human sometimes goes out to get food for his supper.

It was delicious the other evening... my lovely considerate human got take-away fish and chips just like the English ones!

I didn't like fish and chips when I was younger. The concept of hot fish seemed unnatural to me, but I have come around to the idea now.

They always make it too hot to start with, but my human knows this and arranges for my personal portion to cool.

It seems to take a long time, however, and no matter how I fuss and encourage around his legs, the human does not seem able to speed it up.

That said, when served, this dish was at least palatable and not too hot, and I did enjoy it.

My human knows that naturally the chips are of

no interest to me, so he selects the finest parts of the fish just for me, bless him!

Needless to say, I ate it delicately and remembered to leave a little for 'Mr Manners', to make it clear that mere fish, delicious though it was, cannot buy my affections.

However, although annoyingly the door to the patio is mostly shut now that the wind has got up, I did not mind showing my affection and gratitude with a big cuddle as the evening wore on.

I wonder, now that the weather is cooler, if these 'take aways' and warm fish are going to be a more regular thing for my dinner.

I do hope so! It makes a pleasant change.

—-oooOOOooo—-

WHAT WAS HE THINKING?!

After the lovely warm fish the other night, the human has done a very strange thing.

I don't know where he had been hunting, but he bought home the most pungent hot food you could imagine!

It filled the whole domicile with odd odours which linger still, and there was so much of it he has even put some in my fridge, where my cold food comes from!

I sincerely hope he does not expect to give it to me for my breakfast!

When he bought it in, wrapped in brown bags with Indian style writing, he said 'You can't beat a good curry!'
I beg to differ!

I couldn't bear the smell, so I took myself off to the terrace outside and, although there was a cool breeze, there I stayed all evening with just the noisy crickets and the sunset for company.

I had to wait until the all-pervading smell had subsided before I went back in, and although he had not offered any to me ... perhaps as he knew a refusal

was inevitable ... and had prepared a different supper for me, I was quite cross with him.

The scent still lingered early the next morning, but I decided to endure it and allow him to fuss me. At least he did not try to serve any for my breakfast.
I have clearly made my point.

I do hope he does not do it again.

STILL NOISY!

When we first moved to this new abode, I was glad that it was so peaceful. No builders!

But then new people have moved into the apartment above ours.

Bang, Crash, Thump!

Wretched humans! Always mending their things... if they were more careful to start with and didn't break things all the time, they wouldn't need to make such a noise fixing them!

I have a nice thick cushion to hide under which shuts out some of the noise, but my human said they are having air conditioning fitted so the noise might go on for a while.

I remember that from when it was fitted to our villa. They won't like it ... all that cold air blowing at you!

Be quiet, humans! A cat is trying to sleep!

A NEW NORMAL
FOR SILKE

*R*ecently I have started reversing the car round to the front door as my knee is being nasty.
I had to load an old gas bottle up and go to buy a replacement.

Silke followed me out, but sat on the step and would not come any further which, in the circumstances, suited me well. But she was still there on my return.

She saw me coming and belted down the driveway to meet me, I stopped and sure enough she jumped in and we finished reversing together.

By the door she hopped out as if this was an everyday thing.

This charming stuff is quite normal for Silke, bless her!

—-oooOOOooo—-

MEETING BOB
AND BEE

I may have mentioned that our new domicile has, in an outer hallway, stairs leading down to the underground garage where my human parks the car, but there are also steps going up.

My explorations on this higher level revealed nothing much of interest except a curious stout steel gate painted white.

I thought little of it until one day I perceived movement and, glancing up, saw that this gate was open and my keen cat senses told me that, during the night, humans had taken up occupation in whatever lay beyond it.

My cat senses are never wrong, as you would expect, and it was not long before my human noticed these people too.

I waited on the steps when they came out and gave a little chirrup to encourage them to admire me, if they were so minded. It is always my aim to be friendly to the neighbourhood humans and it often pays dividends in terms of treats.

These newcomers were no exception and soon succumbed to my charms, so I contrived to introduce them to my human.

People seem to like my human and he makes friends readily. It may be something to do with his being what I believe you humans call a 'wine merchant' and I have noticed that he regularly hands them bottles of that disgusting drink they all seem to like before they get happy and relaxed in his company.

The same pattern was followed by this new couple from behind the metal gate and we were soon invited in to explore their home.

As is my policy, I looked under all the beds and into each of the rooms after a cursory inspection of the living areas. They seemed tidy enough, so I moved on to explore the wide terrace beyond some glass doors.

There was a table and chairs, as you might expect, and a fine view over the golf course far below (beyond the bridge where the ruffians live) to the sea beyond.

On my second visit the table was set with glasses and some plates and bowls, and once my human had deposited a large box full of bottles in the hall, we were invited to take a seat.

These people, who had introduced themselves as Bob and Bee, came from England it seemed, and I remembered the warm fluffy floors, rustling leaves and soft grass I had so enjoyed on our recent trips there.

As I was musing on these pleasant thoughts the man began to gently stroke me and I realised that, as we had England in common, we could become friends.

The female was fussing with something in the kitchen but then emerged with plates of treats including a selection of sliced meats.

I am normally very wary of this sort of thing as sometimes they are spicy and not to a cat's taste but, now on the man's knee, I could see that these meats may be worthy of further investigation.

The man took a morsel and quite politely offered me some, but my human warned him that I do not like spiced meats, so he should not be offended if I refused the sample.

However, one does not like to be impolite and having decided that this fellow and I could become friends, I leaned forward and took a little bite.

The flavour which filled my mouth was not at all

what I expected. It was delightful, and I was soon back for more. In fact it was so good that, observing how I relished it, my human asked where he could buy some.

I found a soft red cushion on one of the leather sofas in the lounge and, when the breeze got up a little later, I made it my own. From here I could watch the happy humans on the terrace drinking and chatting amiably and I saw that my human had made firm friends with these newcomers.

A few days later, when I returned from a lively debate with the ruffians down by the bridge, my human grabbed me and put stinking stuff on the scratches I had sustained. It stung a lot, and I was very upset with him.

I was not in the mood therefore when, with much ceremony, he unwrapped some spiced ham which he said he had made a special trip to buy just for me.

Call me petulant if you like, but although I recognised it immediately as the same stuff the pleasant people behind the gate had offered me, after a disdainful sniff I strutted, with my nose in the air, onto the balcony.

Cats cannot be bought!

---oooOOOooo---

A CONTENTED LIFE

I am a lucky cat. I live in a perfect place. I love my forever human, I greet him at the door or in the underground garage when he comes home. I know the sound of his car.

Maybe we will travel again in that car soon.

Perhaps one day I might tell you more of my life.

I am a travelling cat but, for now, I am home.

Disclaimer:

Please note: This is a fictional memoir but one which reflects the authors recollections of experiences over a period of time. In order to preserve the anonymity of the people they write about, some names and locations have been changed. Certain individuals are composites, and some events, where they are based in reality, have been created from memory, and in some cases, compressed or adapted to facilitate a natural narrative. The authors accept no claims of any nature.

ABOUT THE AUTHORS

<u>Bob Able</u> is a bestselling writer of popular memoirs, fiction and thrillers. He describes himself as a 'part time ex-pat' splitting his time between his homes in coastal Spain and 'darkest Norfolk' in the UK.

His memoir **'Spain Tomorrow'** was rated as the third most popular travel book by Amazon in September 2020 and continues to top the charts. With the sequel **'More Spain Tomorrow'** these charming lighthearted insights into his life continue to amuse readers.

His works of fiction, **'No Point Running'** and **'The Menace of Blood'** are also written in a lighthearted style, but combine pace and tension with fast moving engaging plots, and he has received many excellent reviews for his work.

All his books are available on the Amazon bookstore as ebooks and paperbacks and can be found by entering **Bob Able** in the search bar or go to:-

www.amazon.com/author/bobable

BOOKS BY
BOB ABLE

<u>Spain Tomorrow</u> - A memoir of an unexpected event and discovering Spain.

When Bob and his long suffering wife Bee unexpectedly inherited just enough money to buy a holiday home in Spain, everything looked rosy. But this was in the middle of the Brexit Referendum chaos; when the UK Government imploded, exchange rates fell through the floor, and nobody knew what the future held.

Was this a sensible time to be buying a property in Spain? Probably not, but Bob and Bee ploughed on anyway!

In this charming and bestselling lighthearted memoir, read how they discovered the delights of the less touristy parts of the Costa Blanca and met a host of wonderful characters, while almost everything in the apartment broke and nobody seemed to know who owned the road!

Ranked in the **top three most popular travel books** by Amazon in September 2020 **'Spain Tomorrow'** continues to top the charts.

---oooOOOooo---

MORE SPAIN
TOMORROW

In this sequel to 'Spain Tomorrow' we follow Bob and Bee on their continuing adventures as 'part time ex-pats'.

But not quite all is fun and laughter for our intrepid pair as there is some devastating news.

Their sense of fun remains undimmed however, as they tackle this new challenge with determination and humour, but a cancer diagnosis is no laughing matter.

This memoir series is an ideal read for anyone contemplating a move to another country, retiring overseas or just buying a holiday home in Spain.

More Spain Tomorrow will entertain and bring a smile to current ex-pats as well as those dreaming of a life in the sun.

A proportion of the royalties from this book is donated to **'The Big C', Norfolk's Cancer Charity**.

---oooOOOooo---

THE MENACE OF BLOOD

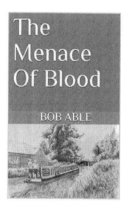

In Spain, Peter leads a busy life, until one morning out of the blue he gets a letter telling him that his long estranged mother has died in England.

What happens next is also unexpected and there is romance, danger, excitement and ultimately a complete surprise in store.

This romantic thriller is not a long book, but it moves at a tremendous pace.

The tension as the plot unfolds makes it difficult to put down.

It takes us from the cozy world of the English country house to the threatening and dangerous world of... well, you had better read it to find out!

---oooOOOooo---

NO POINT RUNNING

'Well, life was simpler in 1978, I suppose you could say. No mobile phones or internet or any of that rot, and Amazon was still just a river. Mind you, that didn't stop me, as a former car thief and telephone sanitiser getting involved, as a guest at a country house with the horse racing set, and almost getting murdered, amongst the highest levels of society; twice.'

In this amusingly written but involving adventure, our narrator has to deal with the consequences of memory loss while trying to start a new life away from crime.

He is nursed back to health by the strikingly lovely Annabelle after taking a beating from his former underworld associates.

Having been given a chance to start afresh we see his old life rearing it's ugly head.
What results is a fast paced thriller with many twists and turns, as he tries to avoid being killed and discover what is driving the much bigger plot to destroy his new life.

Set amongst the world of horse racing and in the society of barristers, upper class layabouts, gardeners, builders and bookies, with more than a hint of romance, this must read novel is written with a lighthearted touch, but packs a punch.

If you remember the 1970's you will love the setting of this book, and if not, you will enjoy a glimpse into a simpler way of life when mobile phones were 'car phones' and only for the rich, and fax machines were a novelty.

---oooOOOooo---

Graham Austin.

Leaving behind his travels in the Bahamas and the USA, where he learned to fly, Graham finally settled in Spain and restored a spectacular villa in one of the better areas of the Costa Blanca.

After a successful career in the world of motor trade warranties and with a well developed interest and no little expertise in the wine industry, Graham continued to travel in Europe and occasionally, when his passion for exotic and vintage motor cars called for it, to the USA.

But it was in Spain, and somewhat unexpectedly that a probably feral but disarmingly charming little black cat came into his life.

He kept detailed chronicles of his life with this adorable little creature, and was easily convinced to work with Bob Able to turn them into a book.

The glorious villa which was so key to this story is still in his ownership and now discerning holiday makers can live like Silke renting it for the summer or just for shorter breaks.

See the advertisement in the back of this book for details.

---oooOOOooo---

Silke the cat.

Time for some thanks, I think ….
Now hold on, I made a list … Ah yes …

Thank you to Rosa the vet for not pricking me recently and protecting me from the dogs in her waiting room while keeping me fit and healthy (You can see her picture, with me in it, at the end of the book).

Thank you to Pedro, old Diego and all my builders for making our villa such an elegant and desirable property.

Thank you to my debating society and the other ruffians down by the bridge for keeping me sharp. Thank you to the man who makes the warm English style fish, and also the chips, which my human likes. Thank you also to Bob and Bee for the spiced ham; I'll be round for some more of that shortly...

Thank you to my mother for giving me this life (cats have nine, you know) and of course to my Forever Human, who I love with all my heart, for making it so special.

And thank you to whoever it was that made my special adventure basket with the cushion on the top, and to our rattly old travelling car for taking us on such wonderful adventures ... but not to Box Woman, she can shut up!

Thank you also to all the kind people I have met on my travels and to those with whom my acquaintance may only have been brief, such as English Gentleman Cat, who bought out my girlish side (such a shame we didn't keep in touch) and Athos the dog at La Folie.
You have all helped to make my life a rich tapestry. I love you all.

But mostly thanks to **you**, my public.

If you keep buying my book and telling all your human friends about it so they can buy it too, my bowl will always be full of the tastiest morsels and I will never again be that broken hearted abandoned little black cat you have so enjoyed reading about.

Silke.

—-oooOOOooo—-

Special acknowledgements

*Thanks to our proof reading and editing team and especially **Angela Potterton** and **Philip Wood** for all their help and advice.*

THANKS FOR READING!

If you enjoyed this book please leave a review on the Amazon bookstore, or on goodreads.com

You can keep in touch with Silke by following her **Facebook page 'Silke the cat'** and email her directly (especially if you are a filmmaker, publisher or media mogul looking to get involved with increasing Silke's profile!) at:-

silkethecat42@gmail.com

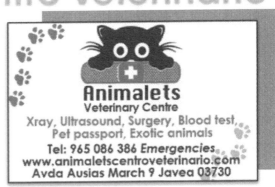

Would you like to stay in Silke's villa?

www.solivillas.com

Villa Tranquila   5 Bedrooms 5 Bathroom sleeps 10

Subject to availability short and long term lets available

VISIT SILKE'S VILLA!

On the magnificent Costa Blanca in Spain

Winter or summer enjoy long or short term holiday rentals
in this spectacular luxury villa.
For availability contact Solivillas:

Liz Kershaw 0034 914 198 047 or 0044 7472954653

liz@solivillas.com who manage the property.

www.solivillas.com

Printed in Poland
by Amazon Fulfillment
Poland Sp. z o.o., Wrocław

68235294R00139